REIGN OF TERROR

The fourth volume of blood-curdling tales of horror from the Victorian era

Also in this series

THE 1ST CORGI BOOK OF GREAT VICTORIAN HORROR STORIES
THE 2ND CORGI BOOK OF GREAT VICTORIAN HORROR STORIES
THE 3RD CORGI BOOK OF GREAT VICTORIAN HORROR STORIES
and coming soon
THE 5TH CORGI BOOK OF GREAT VICTORIAN HORROR STORIES

all edited by Michel Parry and published by Corgi

Edited by Michel Parry

Reign of Terror

The 4th Corgi Book of Great Victorian
Horror Stories

CORGI BOOKS
A DIVISION OF TRANSWORLD PUBLISHERS LTD

REIGN OF TERROR 4

A CORGI BOOK 0 552 10487 6

First publication in Great Britain

PRINTING HISTORY
Corgi edition published 1978

Selection and original material copyright © 1977 by Michel Parry

Corgi books are published by
Transworld Publishers Ltd,
Century House, 61–63 Uxbridge Road,
Ealing, London W5 5SA
Made and printed in Great Britain by
Cox & Wyman Ltd., London, Reading and Fakenham

CONTENTS

	Page
THE STRANGE RIDE OF MORROWBIE JUKES by Rudyard Kipling	9
THE HAUNTED ORGANIST by Rosa Mulholland	37
THE BECKONING HAND by Grant Allen	54
THE DEMON SPELL by Hume Nisbet	87
A MYSTERIOUS VISITOR by Mrs Henry Wood	96
THE LADY ISOPEL by Sir Gilbert Campbell	120
THE WITCHES' SABBATH by James Platt	134
THE SKELETON HAND by Agnes MacLeod	149

ACKNOWLEDGEMENTS

The Editor wishes to thank the following publishers, agents and Estates for their kind permission to reprint copyright material:

A. P. Watt & Son and Mrs George Bambridge for *The Strange Ride of Morrowbie Jukes* by Rudyard Kipling. Reprinted from THE PHANTOM RICKSHAW.

F. V. White & Co. for *The Demon Spell* by Hume Nisbet. Reprinted from THE HAUNTED STATION AND OTHER STORIES (1894).

Ward Lock & Co. Ltd. for *The Lady Isopel* by Sir Gilbert Campbell. Reprinted from MYSTERIES OF THE UNSEEN (1899).

Every effort has been made to ascertain the copyright status of the stories in this collection. In the event of any due acknowledgement being inadvertently omitted, the Editor offers his apologies and expresses his willingness to correct the omission in subsequent editions.

Thanks are due to John Eggling (*Phantasmagoria Books*) and Stanley Nicholls (*Bookends Fantasy Service*) for suggestions and the loan of rare books. And to Martin Walsh for efforts Above and Beyond.

THE STRANGE RIDE OF MORROWBIE JUKES

by Rudyard Kipling

In these cynical times, Rudyard Kipling (1865–1936) has become a rather unfashionable figure, the seeming epitome of Victorian patriotism and the British stiff upper-lip. Yet millions of children continue to be delighted by immortal classics such as the Just So Stories *and the* Jungle Books *(1894–5) just as their fathers secretly relish* Captains Courageous *(1897) and other of Kipling's stirring adventure yarns.*

Kipling was born in Bombay, the son of a connoisseur of Indian art. After an English education, he returned to India as a journalist, filling in his spare time by producing a steady flow of fiction including Plain Tales from the Hills *(1888),* The Phantom Rickshaw, Soldiers Three *and* Under the Deodars. *After a return to England and a marriage (1892), he travelled extensively, living for a time in the United States. In 1900 he covered the Boer War as a reporter and the following year saw the publication of one of his most acclaimed works,* Kim, *which serves as a valuable record of Indian social life and customs of the period. Following this success, Kipling settled in Sussex and became increasingly involved in controversial political issues. His support of conscription and opposition to Votes for Women earned him a reputation as a diehard patriot.*

In later years Kipling turned his hand to drama, writing two plays, The Harbour Watch *(1913) and* The Return of Imray *(1914). He received many awards in recognition of his literary talents, amongst them the Nobel Prize for Literature in 1907 and the gold medal of the Royal Society of Literature in 1926.*

Kipling's ventures into supernatural fiction such as The Mark of the Beast *and* They, *the famous tale of ghostly children, are well-known and much anthologized. Of such stories, Kipling remarked that they were not 'downright ghost stories' but rather 'facts that never explained themselves'.* The Strange Ride of Morrowbie Jukes *has horrors aplenty but of a quite different kind from ghosts.*

Alive or dead – there is no other way. – *Native Proverb.*

THERE is, as the conjurers say, no deception about this tale. Jukes by accident stumbled upon a village that is well known to exist, though he is the only Englishman who has been there. A somewhat similar institution used to flourish on the outskirts of Calcutta, and there is a story that if you go into the heart of Bikanir, which is in the heart of the Great Indian Desert, you shall come across not a village but a town where the Dead who did not die but may not live have established their headquarters. And, since it is perfectly true that in the same Desert is a wonderful city where all the rich moneylenders retreat after they have made their fortunes (fortunes so vast that the owners cannot trust even the strong hand of the Government to protect them, but take refuge in the waterless sands), and drive sumptuous C-spring barouches, and buy beautiful girls and decorate their palaces with gold and ivory and Minton tiles and mother-o'-pearl, I do not see why Jukes's tale should not be true. He is a Civil Engineer, with a head for plans and distances and things of that kind, and he certainly would not take the trouble to invent imaginary traps. He could earn more by doing his legitimate work. He never varies the tale in the telling, and grows very hot and indignant when he thinks of the disrespectful treatment he received. He wrote this quite straightforwardly at first, but he has since touched it up in places and introduced Moral Reflections, thus:

In the beginning it all arose from a slight attack of fever. My work necessitated my being in camp for some months between Pakpattan and Mubarakpur – a desolate sandy stretch of country as every one who has had the misfortune to go there may know. My coolies were neither more nor less exasperating than other gangs, and my work demanded sufficient attention to keep me from moping, had I been inclined to so unmanly a weakness.

On the 23rd December, 1884, I felt a little feverish. There was a full moon at the time, and, in consequence, every dog near my tent was baying it. The brutes assembled in twos and threes and drove me frantic. A few days previously I had shot one loud-mouthed singer and suspended his carcass *in terrorem* about fifty yards from my tent-door. But his friends fell upon, fought for, and ultimately devoured the body: and, as it seemed to me, sang their hymns of thanksgiving afterwards with renewed energy.

The light-headedness which accompanies fever acts differently on different men. My irritation gave way, after a short time, to a fixed determination to slaughter one huge black and white beast who had been foremost in song and first in flight throughout the evening. Thanks to a shaking hand and a giddy head I had already missed him twice with both barrels of my shotgun, when it struck me that my best plan would be to ride him down in the open and finish him off with a hog-spear. This, of course, was merely the semi-delirious notion of a fever patient; but I remember that it struck me at the time as being eminently practical and feasible.

I therefore ordered my groom to saddle Pornic and bring him round quietly to the rear of my tent. When the pony was ready, I stood at his head prepared to mount and dash out as soon as the dog should again lift up his voice. Pornic, by the way, had not been out of his pickets for a couple of days; the night air was crisp and chilly; and I was armed with a specially long and sharp pair of persuaders with which I had been rousing a sluggish cob that afternoon. You will easily believe, then, that when he was let go he went quickly. In one moment, for the brute bolted as straight as a die, the tent was left far behind, and we were flying over the smooth sandy soil at racing speed. In another we had passed the wretched dog, and I had almost forgotten why it was that I had taken horse and hog-spear.

The delirium of fever and the excitement of rapid motion through the air must have taken away the remnant of my senses. I have a faint recollection of standing upright in my stirrups, and of brandishing my hog-spear at the great white Moon that looked down so calmly on my mad gallop; and of shouting challenges to the camel-thorn bushes as they whizzed past. Once or twice, I believe, I swayed forward on Pornic's neck, and literally hung on by my spurs – as the marks next morning showed.

The wretched beast went forward like a thing possessed, over what seemed to be a limitless expanse of moonlit sand. Next, I remember, the ground rose suddenly in front of us, and as we topped the ascent I saw the waters of the Sutlej shining like a silver bar below. Then Pornic blundered heavily on his nose, and we rolled together down some unseen slope.

I must have lost consciousness, for when I recovered I was lying on my stomach in a heap of soft white sand, and the dawn was beginning to break dimly over the edge of the slope down which I had fallen. As the light grew stronger I saw that I was at the bottom of a horseshoe-shaped crater of sand, opening on one side directly on to the shoals of the Sutlej. My fever had altogether left me, and, with the exception of a slight dizziness in the head, I felt no bad effects from the fall over night.

Pornic, who was standing a few yards away, was naturally a good deal exhausted, but had not hurt himself in the least. His saddle, a favourite polo one, was much knocked about, and had been twisted under his belly. It took me some time to put him to rights, and in the meantime I had ample opportunities of observing the spot into which I had so foolishly dropped.

At the risk of being considered tedious, I must describe it at length; inasmuch as an accurate mental picture of its peculiarities will be of material assistance in enabling the reader to understand what follows.

Imagine then, as I have said before, a horseshoe-shaped crater of sand with steeply graded sand walls about thirty-five feet high. (The slope, I fancy, must have been about 65°.) This crater enclosed a level piece of ground about fifty yards long by thirty at its broadest part, with a rude well in the centre. Round the bottom of the crater, about three feet from the level of the ground proper, ran a series of eighty-three semi-circular, ovoid, square, and multilateral holes, all about three feet at the mouth. Each hole on inspection showed that it was carefully shored internally with driftwood and bamboos, and over the mouth a wooden dripboard projected, like the peak of a jockey's cap, for two feet.

No sign of life was visible in these tunnels, but a most sickening stench pervaded the entire amphitheatre – a stench fouler than any which my wanderings in Indian villages have introduced me to.

Having remounted Pornic, who was as anxious as I to get back to camp, I rode round the base of the horseshoe to find some place whence an exit would be practicable. The inhabitants, whoever they might be, had not thought fit to put in any appearance, so I was left to my own devices. My first attempts to 'rush' Pornic up the steep sand-banks showed me that I had fallen into a trap exactly on the same model as that which the ant-lion sets for its prey. At each step the shifting sand poured down from above in tons, and rattled on the drip-boards of the holes like small shot. A couple of ineffectual charges sent us both rolling down to the bottom, half choked with the torrents of sand; and I was constrained to turn my attention to the river-bank.

Here everything seemed easy enough. The sand hills ran down to the river edge, it is true, but there were plenty of shoals and shallows across which I could gallop Pornic, and find my way back to *terra firma* by turning sharply to the right or the left. As I led Pornic over the sands I was startled by the faint pop of a rifle across the river; and at the same moment a bullet dropped with a sharp '*whit*' close to Pornic's head.

There was no mistaking the nature of the missile – a regulation Martini-Henry 'picket'. About five hundred yards away a country-boat was anchored in midstream; and a jet of smoke drifting away from its bows in the still morning air showed me whence the delicate attention had come. Was ever a respectable gentleman in such an *impasse*? The treacherous sand slope allowed no escape from a spot which I had visited most involuntarily, and a promenade on the river frontage was the signal for a bombardment from some insane native in a boat. I'm afraid that I lost my temper very much indeed.

Another bullet reminded me that I had better save my breath to cool my porridge; and I retreated hastily up the sand and back to the horseshoe, where I saw that the noise of the rifle had drawn sixty-five human beings from the badger-holes which I had up till that point supposed to be untenanted. I found myself in the midst of a crowd of spectators – about forty men, twenty women, and one child who could not have been more than five years old. They were all scantily clothed in that salmon-coloured cloth which one associates with Hindu mendicants, and, at first sight, gave me the impression of a band of loathsome *fakirs*. The filth and repulsiveness of the assembly were beyond all description, and I shuddered to think what their life in the badger-holes must be.

Even in these days, when local self-government has destroyed the greater part of a native's respect for a Sahib, I have been accustomed to a certain amount of civility from my inferiors, and on approaching the crowd naturally expected that there would be some recognition of my presence. As a matter of fact there was; but it was by no means what I had looked for.

The ragged crew actually laughed at me – such laughter I hope I may never hear again. They cackled, yelled, whistled, and howled as I walked into their midst; some of them literally throwing themselves down on the ground in convulsions of unholy mirth. In a moment I had let go Pornic's head, and, irritated beyond expression at the morning's adventure, commenced cuffing those nearest to me with all the force I could. The wretches dropped under my blows like nine-pins, and the laughter gave place to wails for mercy; while those yet untouched clasped me round the knees, imploring me in all sorts of uncouth tongues to spare them.

In the tumult, and just when I was feeling very much ashamed of myself for having thus easily given way to my temper, a thin, high voice murmured in English from behind my shoulder: 'Sahib! Sahib! Do you not know me? Sahib, it is Gunga Dass, the telegraph-master.'

I spun round quickly and faced the speaker.

Gunga Dass (I have, of course, no hesitation in mentioning the man's real name) I had known four years before as a Deccanee Brahmin lent by the Punjab Government to one of the Khalsia States. He was in charge of a branch telegraph-office there, and when I had last met him was a jovial, full-stomached, portly Government servant with a marvellous capacity for making bad puns in English – a peculiarity which made me remember him long after I had forgotten his services to me in his official capacity. It is seldom that a Hindu makes English puns.

Now, however, the man was changed beyond all recognition. Caste-mark, stomach, slate-coloured continuations, and unctuous speech were all gone. I looked at a withered skeleton, turbanless and almost naked, with long matted hair and deep-set codfish-eyes. But for a crescent-shaped scar on the left cheek – the result of an accident for which I was responsible – I should never have known him. But it was indubitably Gunga Dass, and – for this I was thankful – an English-speaking native who might at least tell me the meaning of all that I had gone through that day.

The crowd retreated to some distance as I turned towards the miserable figure, and ordered him to show me some method of escaping from the crater. He held a freshly plucked crow in his hand, and in reply to my question climbed slowly on a platform of sand which ran in front of the holes, and commenced lighting a fire there in silence. Dried bents, sand-poppies, and drift-wood burn quickly; and I derived much consolation from the fact that he lit them with an ordinary sulphur-match. When they were in a bright glow, and the crow was neatly spitted in front thereof, Gunga Dass began without a word of preamble:

'There are only two kinds of men, Sar. The alive and the dead. When you are dead you are dead, but when you are alive you live.' (Here the crow demanded his attention for an instant as it twirled before the fire in danger of being burnt to a cinder.) 'If you die at home and do not die when you come to the ghât to be burnt you come here.'

The nature of the reeking village was made plain now, and all that I had known or read of the grotesque and the horrible paled before the fact just communicated by the ex-Brahmin. Sixteen years ago, when I first landed in Bombay, I had been told by a wandering Armenian of the existence, somewhere in India, of a place to which such Hindus as had the misfortune to recover from trance or catalepsy were conveyed and kept, and I recollect laughing heartily at what I was then pleased to consider a traveller's tale. Sitting at the bottom of the sand-trap, the memory of Watson's Hotel, with its swinging punkahs, white-robed attendants, and the sallow-faced Armenian, rose up in my mind as vividly as a photograph, and I burst into a loud fit of laughter. The contrast was too absurd!

Gunga Dass, as he bent over the unclean bird, watched me curiously. Hindus seldom laugh, and his surroundings were not such as to move Gunga Dass to any undue excess of hilarity. He removed the crow solemnly from the wooden spit and as solemnly devoured it. Then he continued his story, which I give in his own words:

'In epidemics of the cholera you are carried to be burnt almost before you are dead. When you come to the riverside the cold air, perhaps, makes you alive, and then, if you are only little alive, mud is put on your nose and mouth and you die conclusively. If you are rather more alive, more mud is put; but if you are too lively they let you go and take you away. I was too lively, and made protestation with anger against the indignities that they endeavoured to press upon me. In those days I was Brahmin and proud man. Now I am dead man and eat' – here he eyed the well-gnawed breast bone with the first sign of emotion that I had seen in him since we met – 'crows, and other things. They took me from my sheets when they saw that I was too lively and gave me medicines for one week, and I survived successfully. Then they sent me by rail from my place to Okara Station, with a man to take care of me; and at Okara Station we met two other men, and they conducted we three on camels, in the night, from Okara Station to this place, and they propelled me from the top to the bottom, and the other two succeeded, and I have been here ever since two and a half years. Once I was Brahmin and proud man, and now I eat crows.'

'There is no way of getting out?'

'None of what kind at all. When I first came I made experiments frequently and all the others also, but we have always succumbed to the sand which is precipitated upon our heads.'

'But surely,' I broke in at this point, 'the river-front is open, and it is worth while dodging the bullets; while at night'—

I had already matured a rough plan of escape which a natural instinct of selfishness forbade me sharing with Gunga Dass. He, however, divined my unspoken thought almost as soon as it was formed; and, to my intense astonishment, gave vent to a long low chuckle of derision – the laughter, be it understood, of a superior or at least of an equal.

'You will not' – he had dropped the Sir completely after his opening sentence – 'make any escape that way. But you can try. I have tried. Once only.'

The sensation of nameless terror and abject fear which I had in vain attempted to strive against overmastered me completely. My long fast – it was now close upon ten o'clock, and I had eaten nothing since tiffin on the previous day – combined with the violent and unnatural agitation of the ride had exhausted me, and I verily believe that, for a few minutes, I acted as one mad. I hurled myself against the pitiless sand-slope. I ran round the base of the crater, blaspheming and praying by turns. I crawled out among the sedges of the river-front, only to be driven back each time in an agony of nervous dread by the rifle-bullets which cut up the sand round me – for I dared not face the death of a mad dog among that hideous crowd – and finally fell, spent and raving, at the curb of the well. No one had taken the slightest notice of an exhibition which makes me blush hotly even when I think of it now.

Two or three men trod on my panting body as they drew water, but they were evidently used to this sort of thing, and had no time to waste upon me. The situation was humiliating. Gunga Dass, indeed, when he had banked the embers of his fire with sand, was at some pains to throw half a cupful of fetid water over my head, an attention for which I could have fallen on my knees and thanked him, but he was laughing all the while in the same mirthless, wheezy key that greeted me on my first attempt to force the shoals. And so, in a semi-comatose condition, I lay till noon. Then, being only a man after all, I felt hungry, and intimated as much to Gunga Dass, whom I had begun to regard as my natural protector. Following the impulse of the outer world when dealing with natives, I put my hand into my pocket and drew out four annas. The absurdity of the gift struck me at once, and I was about to replace the money.

Gunga Dass, however, was of a different opinion. 'Give me the money,' said he; 'all you have, or I will get help, and we will kill you!' All this as if it were the most natural thing in the world!

A Briton's first impulse, I believe, is to guard the contents of his pockets; but a moment's reflection convinced me of the futility of differing with the one man who had it in his power to make me comfortable; and with whose help it was possible that I might eventually escape from the crater. I gave him all the money in my possession, Rs. 9-8-5 – nine rupees eight annas and five pie – for I always keep small change as *bakshish* when I am in camp. Gunga Dass clutched the coins, and hid them at once in his ragged loincloth, his expression changing to something diabolical as he looked round to assure himself that no one had observed us.

'*Now* I will give you something to eat,' said he.

What pleasure the possession of my money could have afforded him I am unable to say; but inasmuch as it did give him evident delight I was not sorry that I had parted with it so readily, for I had no doubt that he would have had me killed if I had refused. One does not protest against the vagaries of a den of wild beasts; and my companions were lower than any beasts. While I devoured what Gunga Dass had provided, a course *chapatti* and a cupful of the foul well-water, the people showed not the faintest sign of curiosity – that curiosity which is so rampant, as a rule, in an Indian village.

I could even fancy that they despised me. At all events they treated me with the most chilling indifference, and Gunga Dass was nearly as bad. I plied him with questions about the terrible village, and received extremely unsatisfactory answers. So far as I could gather, it had been in existence from time immemorial – whence I concluded that it was at least a century old – and during that time no one had ever been known to escape from it. [I had to control myself here with both hands, lest the blind terror should lay hold of me a second time and drive me raving round the crater.] Gunga Dass took a malicious pleasure in emphasizing this point and in watching me wince. Nothing that I could do would induce him to tell me who the mysterious 'They' were.

'It is so ordered,' he would reply, 'and I do not yet know any one who has disobeyed the orders.'

'Only wait till my servants find that I am missing,' I retorted, 'and I promise you that this place shall be cleared off the face of the earth, and I'll give you a lesson in civility, too, my friend.'

'Your servants would be torn in pieces before they came near this place; and, besides, you are dead, my dear friend. It is not your fault, of course, but none the less you are dead *and* buried.'

At irregular intervals supplies of food, I was told, were dropped down from the land side into the amphitheatre, and the inhabitants fought for them like wild beasts. When a man felt his death coming on he retreated to his lair and died there. The body was sometimes dragged out of the hole and thrown on to the sand, or allowed to rot where it lay.

The phrase 'thrown on to the sand' caught my attention, and I asked Gunga Dass whether this sort of thing was not likely to breed a pestilence.

'That,' said he, with another of his wheezy chuckles, 'you may see for yourself subsequently. You will have much time to make observations.'

Whereat, to his great delight, I winced once more and hastily continued the conversation: 'And how do you live here from day to day? What do you do?' The question elicited exactly the same answer as before – coupled with the information that 'this place is like your European heaven; there is neither marrying nor giving in marriage.'

Gunga Dass had been educated at a Mission School, and,

as he himself admitted, had he only changed his religion 'like a wise man', might have avoided the living grave which was now his portion. But as long as I was with him I fancy he was happy.

Here was a Sahib, a representative of the dominant race, helpless as a child and completely at the mercy of his native neighbours. In a deliberate lazy way he set himself to torture me as a schoolboy would devote a rapturous half-hour to watching the agonies of an impaled beetle, or as a ferret in a blind burrow might glue himself comfortably to the neck of a rabbit. The burden of his conversation was that there was no escape 'of no kind whatever', and that I should stay here till I died and was 'thrown on to the sand'. If it were possible to forejudge the conversation of the Damned on the advent of a new soul in their abode, I should say that they would speak as Gunga Dass did to me throughout that long afternoon. I was powerless to protest or answer; all my energies being devoted to a struggle against the inexplicable terror that threatened to overwhelm me again and again. I can compare the feeling to nothing except the struggles of a man against the overpowering nausea of the Channel passage – only my agony was of the spirit and infinitely more terrible.

As the day wore on, the inhabitants began to appear in full strength to catch the rays of the afternoon sun, which were now sloping in at the mouth of the crater. They assembled in little knots, and talked among themselves without even throwing a glance in my direction. About four o'clock, as far as I could judge, Gunga Dass rose and dived into his lair for a moment, emerging with a live crow in his hands. The wretched bird was in a most draggled and deplorable condition, but seemed to be in no way afraid of its master. Advancing cautiously to the river-front, Gunga Dass stepped from tussock to tussock until he had reached a smooth patch of sand directly in the line of the boat's fire.

The occupants of the boat took no notice. Here he stopped, and, with a couple of dexterous turns of the wrist, pegged the bird on its back with outstretched wings. As was only natural, the crow began to shriek at once and beat the air with its claws. In a few seconds the clamour had attracted the attention of a bevy of wild crows on a shoal a few hundred yards away, where they were discussing something that looked like a corpse. Half a dozen crows flew over at once to see what was going on, and also, as it proved, to attack the pinioned bird. Gunga Dass, who had laid down on a tussock, motioned to me to be quiet, though I fancy this was a needless precaution. In a moment, and before I could see how it happened, a wild crow, who had grappled with the shrieking and helpless bird, was entangled in the latter's claws, swiftly disengaged by Gunga Dass, and pegged down beside its companion in adversity. Curiosity, it seemed, overpowered the rest of the flock, and almost before Gunga Dass and I had time to withdraw to the tussock, two more captives were struggling in the upturned claws of the decoys. So the chase – if I can give it so dignified a name – continued until Gunga Dass had captured seven crows. Five of them he throttled at once, reserving two for further operations another day. I was a good deal impressed by this, to me, novel method of securing food, and complimented Gunga Dass on his skill.

'It is nothing to do,' said he. 'Tomorrow you must do it for me. You are stronger than I am.'

This calm assumption of superiority upset me not a little, and I answered peremptorily; – 'Indeed, you old ruffian! What do you think I have given you money for?'

'Very well,' was the unmoved reply. 'Perhaps not tomorrow, nor the day after, nor subsequently; but in the end, and for many years, you will catch crows and eat crows, and you will thank your European God that you have crows to catch and eat.'

I could have cheerfully strangled him for this; but judged it best under the circumstances to smother my resentment. An hour later I was eating one of the crows; and, as Gunga Dass had said, thanking my God that I had a crow to eat. Never as long as I live shall I forget that evening meal. The whole population were squatting on the hard sand platform opposite their dens, huddled over tiny fires of refuse and dried rushes. Death, having once laid his hand upon these men and forborne to strike, seemed to stand aloof from them now; for most of our company were old men, bent and worn and twisted with years, and women aged to all appearances as the Fates themselves. They sat together in knots and talked – God only knows what they found to discuss – in low equable tones, curiously in contrast to the strident babble with which natives are accustomed to make day hideous. Now and then an access of that sudden fury which had possessed me in the morning would lay hold on a man or woman; and with yells and imprecations the sufferer would attack the steep slope until, baffled and bleeding, he fell back on the platform incapable of moving a limb. The others would never even raise their eyes when this happened, as men too well aware of the futility of their fellows' attempts and wearied with their useless repetition. I saw four such outbursts in the course of that evening.

Gunga Dass took an eminently businesslike view of my situation, and while we were dining – I can afford to laugh at the recollection now, but it was painful enough at the time – propounded the terms on which he would consent to 'do' for me. My nine rupees eight annas, he argued, at the rate of three annas a day, would provide me with food for fifty-one days, or about seven weeks; that is to say, he would be willing to cater for me for that length of time. At the end of it I was to look after myself. For a further consideration – *videlicet* my boots – he would be willing to allow me to occupy the den next to his own, and would supply me with as much dried grass for bedding as he could spare.

'Very well, Gunga Dass,' I replied; 'to the first terms I cheerfully agree, but, as there is nothing on earth to prevent my killing you as you sit here and taking everything that you have' (I thought of the two invaluable crows at the time), 'I flatly refuse to give you my boots and shall take whichever den I please.'

The stroke was a bold one, and I was glad when I saw that it had succeeded. Gunga Dass changed his tone immediately, and disavowed all intention of asking for my boots. At the time it did not strike me as at all strange that I, a Civil Engineer, a man of thirteen years' standing in the Service, and, I trust, an average Englishman, should thus calmly threaten murder and violence against the man who had, for a consideration it is true, taken me under his wing. I had left the world, it seemed, for centuries. I was as certain then as I am now of my own existence, that in the accursed settlement there was no law save that of the strongest; that the living dead men had thrown behind them every canon of the world which had cast them out; and that I had to depend for my own life on my strength and vigilance alone. The crew of the ill-fated Mignonette are the only men who would understand my frame of mind. 'At present,' I argued to myself, 'I am strong and a match for six of these wretches. It is imperatively necessary that I should, for my own sake, keep both health and strength until the hour of my release comes – if it ever does.'

Fortified with these resolutions, I ate and drank as much as I could, and made Gunga Dass understand that I intended to be his master, and that the least sign of insubordination on his part would be visited with the only punishment I had it in my power to inflict – sudden and violent death. Shortly after this I went to bed. That is to say, Gunga Dass gave me a double armful of dried bents which I thrust down the mouth of the lair to the right of his, and followed myself, feet foremost; the hole running about nine feet into the sand with a slight downward inclination, and being neatly shored with timbers. From my den, which faced the river-front, I was able to watch the waters of the Sutlej flowing past under the light of a young moon and compose myself to sleep as best I might.

The horrors of that night I shall never forget. My den was nearly as narrow as a coffin, and the sides had been worn smooth and greasy by the contact of innumerable naked bodies, added to which it smelled abominably. Sleep was altogether out of question to one in my excited frame of mind. As the night wore on, it seemed that the entire amphitheatre was filled with legions of unclean devils that, trooping up from the shoals below, mocked the unfortunates in their lairs.

Personally I am not of an imaginative temperament – very few Engineers are – but on that occasion I was as completely prostrated with nervous terror as any woman. After half an hour or so, however, I was able once more to calmly review my chances of escape. Any exit by the steep sand walls was, of course, impracticable. I had been thoroughly convinced of this some time before. It was possible, just possible, that I might, in the uncertain moonlight, safely run the gauntlet of the rifle shots. The place was so full of terror for me that I was prepared to undergo any risk in leaving it. Imagine my delight, then, when after creeping stealthily to the river-front I found that the infernal boat was not there. My freedom lay before me in the next few steps!

By walking out to the first shallow pool that lay at the foot of the projecting left horn of the horseshoe, I could wade across, turn the flank of the crater, and make my way inland. Without a moment's hesitation I marched briskly past the tussocks where Gunga Dass had snared the crows, and out in the direction of the smooth white sand beyond. My first step from the tufts of dried grass showed me how utterly futile was any hope of escape; for, as I put my foot down, I felt an indescribably drawing, sucking motion of the sand below. Another moment and my leg was swallowed up nearly to the knee. In the moonlight the whole surface of the sand seemed to be shaken with devilish delight at my disappointment. I struggled clear, sweating with terror and exertion, back to the tussocks behind me and fell on my face.

My only means of escape from the semi-circle was protected with a quicksand!

How long I lay I have not the faintest idea; but I was roused at last by the malevolent chuckle of Gunga Dass at my ear. 'I would advise you, Protector of the Poor' (the ruffian was speaking English) 'to return to your house. It is unhealthy to lie down here. Moreover, when the boat returns, you will most certainly be rifled at.' He stood over me in the dim light of the dawn, chuckling and laughing to himself. Suppressing my first impulse to catch the man by the neck and throw him onto the quicksand, I rose sullenly and followed him to the platform below the burrows.

Suddenly, and futilely as I thought while I spoke, I asked: 'Gunga Dass, what is the good of the boat if I can't get out *anyhow*?' I recollect that even in my deepest trouble I had been speculating vaguely on the waste of ammunition in guarding an already well protected foreshore.

Gunga Dass laughed again and made answer: 'They have the boat only in daytime. It is for the reason that *there is a way*. I hope we shall have the pleasure of your company for much longer time. It is a pleasant spot when you have been here some years and eaten roast crow long enough.'

I staggered, numbed and helpless, towards the fetid burrow allotted to me, and fell asleep. An hour or so later I was awakened by a piercing scream – the shrill, high-pitched scream of a horse in pain. Those who have once heard that will never forget the sound. I found some little difficulty in scrambling out of the burrow. When I was in the open, I saw Pornic, my poor old Pornic, lying dead on the sandy soil. How they had killed him I cannot guess. Gunga Dass explained that horse was better than crow, and 'greatest good of greatest number is political maxim. We are now Republic, Mister Jukes, and you are entitled to a fair share of the beast. If you like, we will pass a vote of thanks. Shall I propose?'

Yes, we were a Republic indeed! A Republic of wild beasts penned at the bottom of a pit, to eat and fight and sleep till we died. I attempted no protest of any kind, but sat down and stared at the hideous sight in front of me. In less time almost than it takes me to write this, Pornic's body was divided, in some unclean way or other; the men and women had dragged the fragments on to the platform and were preparing their morning meal. Gunga Dass cooked mine. The almost irresistible impulse to fly at the sand walls until I was wearied laid hold of me afresh, and I had to struggle against it with all my might. Gunga Dass was offensively jocular till I told him that if he addressed another remark of any kind whatever to me I should strangle him where he sat. This silenced him till silence became insupportable, and I bade him say something.

'You will live here till you die like the other Feringhi,' he said coolly, watching me over the fragment of gristle that he was gnawing.

'What other Sahib, you swine? Speak at once, and don't stop to tell me a lie.'

'He is over there,' answered Gunga Dass, pointing to a burrow-mouth about four doors to the left of my own. 'You can see for yourself. He died in the burrow as you will die, and I will die; and as all these men and women and the one child will also die.'

'For pity's sake tell me all you know about him. Who was he? When did he come, and when did he die?'

This appeal was a weak step on my part. Gunga Dass only leered and replied: 'I will not – unless you give me something first.'

Then I recollected where I was, and struck the man between the eyes, partially stunning him. He stepped down from the platform at once, and, cringing and fawning and weeping and attempting to embrace my feet, led me round to the burrow which he had indicated.

'I know nothing whatever about the gentleman. Your God be my witness that I do not. He was as anxious to escape as you were, and he was shot from the boat, though we all did all things to prevent him from attempting. He was shot here.' Gunga Dass laid his hand on his lean stomach and bowed to the earth.

'Well, and what then? Go on!'

'And then – and then, Your Honour, we carried him in to his house and gave him water, and put wet clothes on the wound, and he laid down in his house and gave up the ghost.'

'In how long? In how long?'

'About half an hour, after he received his wound. I call Vishru to witness,' yelled the wretched man, 'that I did everything for him. Everything which was possible, that I did!'

He threw himself down on the ground and clasped my ankles. But I had my doubts about Gunga Dass's benevolence, and kicked him off as he lay protesting.

'I believe you robbed him of everything he had. But I can find out in a minute or two. How long was the Sahib here?'

'Nearly a year and a half. I think he must have gone mad. But hear me swear, Protector of the Poor! Won't Your

Honour hear me swear that I never touched an article that belonged to him? What is Your Worship going to do?'

I had taken Gunga Dass by the waist and had hauled him on to the platform opposite the deserted burrow. As I did so I thought of my wretched fellow-prisoner's unspeakable misery among all these horrors for eighteen months, and the final agony of dying like a rat in a hole, with a bullet-wound in the stomach. Gunga Dass fancied I was going to kill him and howled pitifully. The rest of the population, in the plethora that follows a full flesh meal, watched us without stirring.

'Go inside, Gunga Dass,' said I, 'and fetch it out.'

I was feeling sick and faint with horror now. Gunga Dass nearly rolled off the platform and howled aloud.

'But I am Brahmin, Sahib – a high-caste Brahmin. By your soul, by your father's soul, do not make me do this thing!'

'Brahmin or no Brahmin, by my soul and my father's soul, in you go!' I said, and, seizing him by the shoulders, I crammed his head into the mouth of the burrow, kicked the rest of him in, and, sitting down, covered my face with my hands.

At the end of a few minutes I heard a rustle and a creak; then Gunga Dass in a sobbing, choking whisper speaking to himself; then a soft thud – and I uncovered my eyes.

The dry sand had turned the corpse entrusted to its keeping into a yellow-brown mummy. I told Gunga Dass to stand off while I examined it. The body – clad in an olive-green hunting-suit much stained and worn, with leather pads on the shoulders – was that of a man between thirty and forty, above middle height, with light, sandy hair, long moustache, and a rough unkempt beard. The left canine of the upper jaw was missing, and a portion of the lobe of the right ear was gone. On the second finger of the left hand was a ring – a shield-shaped bloodstone set in gold, with a monogram that might have been either 'B.K.' or 'B.L.'. On the third finger of the right hand was a silver ring in the shape of a coiled cobra, much worn and tarnished. Gunga Dass deposited a handful of trifles he had picked out of the burrow at my feet, and, covering the face of the body with my handkerchief, I turned to examine these. I give the full list in the hope that it may lead to the identification of the unfortunate man:

1. Bowl of a briarwood pipe, serrated at the edge; much worn and blackened; bound with string at the screw.

2. Two patent-lever keys; wards of both broken.

3. Tortoise-shell-handled penknife, silver or nickel, name-plate, marked with monogram 'B.K'.

4. Envelope, post-mark undecipherable, being a Victorian stamp, addressed to 'Miss Mon—' (rest illegible) –'ham' – 'nt'.

5. Imitation crocodile-skin note-book with pencil. First forty-five pages blank; four and a half illegible; fifteen others filled with private memoranda relating chiefly to three persons – a Mrs. L. Singleton, abbreviated several times to 'Lot Single', 'Mrs. S. May', and 'Garmison', referred to in places as 'Jerry' or 'Jack'.

6. Handle of small-sized hunting-knife. Blade snapped short. Buck's horn, diamond-cut, with swivel and ring on the butt; fragment of cotton cord attached.

It must not be supposed that I inventoried all these things on the spot as fully as I have here written them down. The note-book first attracted my attention, and I put it in my pocket with a view to studying it later on. The rest of the articles I conveyed to my burrow for safety's sake, and there, being a methodical man, I inventoried them. I then returned to the corpse and ordered Gunga Dass to help me to carry it out to the river-front. While we were engaged in this, the exploded shell of an old brown cartridge dropped out of one of the pockets and rolled at my feet. Gunga Dass had not seen it; and I fell to thinking that a man does not carry exploded cartridge-cases, especially 'browns', which will not bear loading twice, about with him when shooting. In other words, that cartridge-case had been fired inside the crater. Consequently there must be a gun somewhere. I was on the verge of asking Gunga Dass, but checked myself, knowing that he would lie. We laid the body down on the edge of the quicksand by the tussocks. It was my intention to push it out and let it be swallowed up – the only possible mode of burial that I could think of. I ordered Gunga Dass to go away.

Then I gingerly put the corpse out on the quicksand. In doing so, it was lying face downward, I tore the frail and rotten khaki shooting-coat open, disclosing a hideous cavity in the back. I have already told you that the dry sand had, as it were, mummified the body. A moment's glance showed that the gaping hole had been caused by a gunshot wound; the gun must have been fired with the muzzle almost touching the back. The shooting-coat, being intact, had been drawn over the body after death, which must have been instantaneous. The secret of the poor wretch's death was plain to me in a flash. Some one of the crater, presumably Gunga Dass, must have shot him with his own gun – the gun that fitted the brown cartridges. He had never attempted to escape in the face of the rifle-fire from the boat.

I pushed the corpse out hastily, and saw it sink from sight literally in a few seconds. I shuddered as I watched. In a dazed, half-conscious way I turned to peruse the notebook. A stained and discoloured slip of paper had been inserted between the binding and the back; and dropped out as I opened the pages. This is what it contained: *'Four out from crow-clump: three left; nine out; two right; three back; two left; fourteen out; two left; seven out; one left; nine back;*

two right; six back; four right; seven back.' The paper had been burnt and charred at the edges. What it meant I could not understand. I sat down on the dried bents turning it over and over between my fingers, until I was aware of Gunga Dass standing immediately behind me with glowing eyes and outstretched hands.

'Have you got it?' he panted. 'Will you not let me look at it also? I swear that I will return it.'

'Got what? Return what?' I asked.

'That which you have in your hands. It will help us both.' He stretched out his long, bird-like talons, trembling with eagerness.

'I could never find it,' he continued. 'He had secreted it about his person. Therefore I shot him, but nevertheless I was unable to obtain it.'

Gunga Dass had quite forgotten his little fiction about the rifle-bullet. I received the information perfectly calmly. Morality is blunted by consorting with the Dead who are alive.

'What on earth are you raving about? What is it you want me to give you?'

'The piece of paper in the note-book. It will help us both. Oh, you fool! You fool! Can you not see what it will do for us? We shall escape!'

His voice rose almost to a scream, and he danced with excitement before me. I own I was moved at the chance of getting away.

'Don't skip! Explain yourself. Do you mean to say that this slip of paper will help us? What does it mean?'

'Read it aloud! Read it aloud! I beg and I pray to you to read it aloud.'

I did so. Gunga Dass listened delightedly, and drew an irregular line in the sand with his fingers.

'See now! It was the length of his gun-barrels without the

stock. I have those barrels. Four gun-barrels out from the place where I caught crows. Straight out do you follow me? Then three left – Ah! how well I remember when that man worked it out night after night. Then nine out, and so on. Out is always straight before you across the quicksand. He told me so before I killed him.'

'But if you knew all this why didn't you get out before?'

'I did *not* know it. He told me that he was working it out a year and a half ago, and how he was working it out night after night when the boat had gone away, and he could get out near the quicksand safely. Then he said that we would get away together. But I was afraid that he would leave me behind one night when he had worked it all out, and so I shot him. Besides, it is not advisable that the men who once get in here should escape. Only I, and *I* am a Brahmin.'

The prospect of escape had brought Gunga Dass's caste back to him. He stood up, walked about and gesticulated violently. Eventually I managed to make him talk soberly, and he told me how this Englishman had spent six months night after night in exploring, inch by inch, the passage across the quicksand; how he had declared it to be simplicity itself up to within about twenty yards of the river bank after turning the flank of the left horn of the horseshoe. This much he had evidently not completed when Gunga Dass shot him with his own gun.

In my frenzy of delight at the possibilities of escape I recollect shaking hands effusively with Gunga Dass, after we had decided that we were to make an attempt to get away that very night. It was weary work waiting throughout the afternoon.

About ten o'clock, as far as I could judge, when the Moon had just risen above the lip of the crater, Gunga Dass made a move for his burrow to bring out the gun-barrels whereby to measure our path. All the other wretched inhabitants had retired to their lairs long ago. The guardian boat drifted downstream some hours before, and we were utterly alone by the crow-clump. Gunga Dass, while carrying the gun-barrels, let slip the piece of paper which was to be our guide. I stooped down hastily to recover it, and, as I did so, I was aware that the diabolical Brahmin was aiming a violent blow at the back of my head with the gun-barrels. It was too late to turn round. I must have received the blow somewhere on the nape of my neck. A hundred thousand fiery stars danced before my eyes, and I fell forward senseless at the edge of the quicksand.

When I recovered consciousness, the Moon was going down, and I was sensible of intolerable pain in the back of my head. Gunga Dass had disappeared and my mouth was full of blood. I lay down again and prayed that I might die without more ado. Then the unreasoning fury which I have before mentioned laid hold upon me, and I staggered inland towards the walls of the crater. It seemed that some one was calling to me in a whisper – 'Sahib! Sahib! Sahib!' exactly as my bearer used to call me in the mornings. I fancied that I was delirious until a handful of sand fell at my feet. Then I looked up and saw a head peering down into the amphitheatre – the head of Dunnoo, my dog-boy, who attended to my collies. As soon as he had attracted my attention, he held up his hand and showed a rope. I motioned, staggering to and fro the while, that he should throw it down. It was a couple of leather punkah-ropes knotted together, with a loop at one end. I slipped the loop over my head and under my arms; heard Dunnoo urge something forward; was conscious that I was being dragged, face downward, up the steep sand slope, and the next instant found myself choked and half fainting on the sand hills overlooking the crater. Dunnoo, with his face ashy grey in the moonlight, implored me not to stay but to get back to my tent at once.

It seems that he had tracked Pornic's footprints fourteen miles across the sands to the crater; had returned and told my servants, who flatly refused to meddle with any one, white or black, once fallen into the hideous Village of the Dead; whereupon Dunnoo had taken one of my ponies and a couple of punkah ropes, returned to the crater, and hauled me out as I have described.

To cut a long story short, Dunnoo is now my personal servant on a gold mohur a month – a sum which I still think far too little for the services he has rendered. Nothing on earth will induce me to go near that devilish spot again, or to reveal its whereabouts more clearly than I have done. Of Gunga Dass I have never found a trace, nor do I wish to do. My sole motive in giving this to be published is the hope that some one may possibly identify, from the details and the inventory which I have given above, the corpse of the man in the olive-green hunting-suit.

THE HAUNTED ORGANIST

by Rosa Mulholland

Like many another writer of weird stories, Rosa Mulholland was Irish and proud of it for she wrote biographies of prominent Irishmen and collected Irish stories for publication. She also wrote verse, fairy tales for children, and is credited with several novels, chiefly Cousin Sara; The Daughter in Possession *and one with the fine gothic-sounding title of* Banshee Castle (1894.) *In 1891 she became Lady Rosa Gilbert following her marriage to Sir John Thomas Gilbert. She died in 1921.*

THERE had been a thunderstorm in the village of Hurly Burly. Every door was shut, every dog in his kennel, every rut and gutter a flowing river after the deluge of rain that had fallen. Up at the great house, a mile from the town, the rooks were calling to one another about the fright they had been in, the fawns in the deer-park were venturing their timid heads from behind the trunks of trees, and the old woman at the gate-lodge had risen from her knees, and was putting back her prayer-book on the shelf. In the garden, July roses, unwieldy with their full-blown richness, and saturated with rain, hung their heads heavily to the earth; others, already fallen, lay flat upon their blooming faces on the path, where Bess, Mistress Hurly's maid, would find them, when going on her morning quest of rose-leaves for her lady's potpourri. Ranks of white lilies, just brought to perfection by to-day's sun, lay dabbled in the mire of flooded mould. Tears ran down the amber cheeks of the plums on the south wall, and not a bee had ventured out of the hives, though the scent of the air was sweet enough to tempt the laziest drone. The sky was still lurid behind the boles of the upland oaks, but the birds had begun to dive in and out of the ivy that wrapped up the home of the Hurlys of Hurly Burly.

This thunderstorm took place more than half a century ago, and we must remember that Mistress Hurly was dressed in the fashion of that time as she crept out from behind the squire's chair, now that the lightning was over, and, with many nervous glances towards the window, sat down before her husband, the tea-urn, and the muffins. We can picture her fine lace cap, with its peachy ribbons, the frill on the hem of her cambric gown just touching her ankles, the embroidered clocks on her stockings, the rosettes on her shoes, but not so easily the lilac shade of her mild eyes, the satin skin, which still kept its delicate bloom, though wrinkled with advancing age, and the pale, sweet, puckered mouth, that time and sorrow had made angelic while trying vainly to deface its beauty.

The squire was as rugged as his wife was gentle, his skin as brown as hers was white, his grey hair as bristling as hers was glossed; the years had ploughed his face into ruts and channels; a bluff, choleric, noisy man he had been; but of late a dimness had come on his eyes, a hush on his loud voice, and a check on the spring of his hale step. He looked at his wife often, and very often she looked at him. She was not a tall woman, and he was only a head higher. They were a quaintly well-matched couple, despite their differences.

She turned to you with nervous sharpness and revealed her tender voice and eye; he spoke and glanced roughly, but the turn of his head was courteous. Of late they fitted one another better than they had ever done in the heyday of their youthful love. A common sorrow had developed a singular likeness between them. In former years the cry from the wife had been, 'Don't curb my son too much!' and from the husband, 'You ruin the lad with softness.' But now the idol that had stood between them was removed, and they saw each other better.

The room in which they sat was a pleasant old-fashioned drawing-room, with a general spider-legged character about the fittings; spinet and guitar in their places, with a great deal of copied music beside them; carpet, tawny wreaths on pale blue; blue flutings on the walls, and faint gilding on the furniture. A huge urn, crammed with roses, in the open bay-window, through which came delicious airs from the garden, the twittering of birds settling to sleep in the ivy close by, and occasionally the pattering of a flight of rain-drops, swept to the ground as a bough bent in the breeze. The urn on the table was ancient silver, and the china rare. There was nothing in the room for luxurious ease of the body, but everything of delicate refinement for the eye.

There was a great hush all over Hurly Burly, except in the neighbourhood of the rooks. Every living thing had suffered from heat for the past month, and now, in common with all Nature, was receiving the boon of refreshed air in silent peace. The mistress and master of Hurly Burly shared the general spirit that was abroad, and were not talkative over their tea.

'Do you know,' said Mistress Hurly, at last, 'when I heard the first of the thunder beginning I thought it was – it was—'

The lady broke down, her lips trembling, and the peachy ribbons of her cap stirring with great agitation.

'Pshaw!' cried the old squire, making his cup suddenly ring upon the saucer, 'we ought to have forgotten that. Nothing has been heard for three months.'

At this moment a rolling sound struck upon the ears of both. The lady rose from her seat trembling, and folded her hands together, while the tea-urn flooded the tray.

'Nonsense, my love,' said the squire; 'that is the noise of wheels. Who can be arriving?'

'Who, indeed?' murmured the lady, reseating herself in agitation.

Presently pretty Bess of the rose-leaves appeared at the door in a flutter of blue ribbons.

'Please, madam, a lady has arrived, and says she is expected. She asked for her apartment, and I put her into the room that was got ready for Miss Calderwood. And she sends her respects to you, madam, and she'll be down with you presently.'

The squire looked at his wife, and his wife looked at the squire.

'It is some mistake,' murmured madam. 'Some visitor for Calderwood or the Grange. It is very singular.'

Hardly had she spoken when the door again opened, and the stranger appeared – a small creature, whether girl or woman it would be hard to say – dressed in a scanty black silk dress, her narrow shoulders covered with a white muslin pelerine. Her hair was swept up to the crown of her head, all but a little fringe hanging over her low forehead within an inch of her brows. Her face was brown and thin, eyes black and long, with blacker settings, mouth large, sweet, and melancholy. She was all head, mouth, and eyes; her nose and chin were nothing.

This visitor crossed the floor hastily, dropped a curtsey in the middle of the room, and approached the table, saying abruptly, with a soft Italian accent:

'Sir and madam, I am here. I am come to play your organ.'

'The organ!' gasped Mistress Hurly.

'The organ!' stammered the squire.

'Yes, the organ,' said the little stranger lady, playing on the back of a chair with her fingers, as if she felt notes under them. 'It was but last week that the handsome signor, your son, came to my little house, where I have lived teaching music since my English father and my Italian mother and brothers and sisters died and left me so lonely.'

Here the fingers left off drumming, and two great tears were brushed off, one from each eye with each hand, child's fashion. But the next moment the fingers were at work again, as if only whilst they were moving the tongue could speak.

'The noble signor, your son,' said the little woman, looking trustfully from one to the other of the old couple, while a bright blush shone through her brown skin, 'he often came to see me before that, always in the evening, when the sun was warm and yellow all through my little studio, and the music was swelling my heart, and I could play out grand with all my soul; then he used to come and say, "Hurry, little Lisa, and play better, better still. I have work for you to do by-and-by." Sometimes he said, "Brava!" and sometimes he said "Eccellentissima!" but one night last week he came to me and said, "It is enough. Will you swear to do my bidding, whatever it may be?" Here the black eyes fell. And I said, "Yes." And he said, "Now you are my betrothed." "And I said, "Yes." And he said, "Pack up your music, little Lisa, and go off to England to my English father and mother, who have an organ in their house which must be played upon. If they refuse to let you play, tell them I sent you, and they will give you leave. You must play all day, and you must get up in the night and play. You must never tire. You are my betrothed, and you have sworn to do my work." I said, "Shall I see you there, signor?" And he said, "Yes, you shall see me there." I said, "I will keep my vow, signor." And so, sir and madam, I am come.'

The soft foreign voice left off talking, the fingers left off thrumming on the chair, and the little stranger gazed in dismay at her auditors, both pale with agitation.

'You are deceived. You make a mistake,' said they in one breath.

'Our son—' began Mistress Hurly, but her mouth twitched, her voice broke, and she looked piteously towards her husband.

'Our son,' said the squire, making an effort to conquer the quavering in his voice, 'our son is long dead.'

'Nay, nay,' said the little foreigner. 'If you have thought him dead have good cheer, dear sir and madam. He is alive; he is well, and strong, and handsome. But one, two, three, four, five' (on the fingers) 'days ago he stood by my side.'

'It is some strange mistake, some wonderful coincidence!' said the mistress and master of Hurly Burly.

'Let us take her to the gallery,' murmured the mother of this son who was thus dead and alive. 'There is yet light to see the pictures. She will not know his portrait.'

The bewildered wife and husband led their strange visitor away to a long gloomy room at the west side of the house, where the faint gleams from the darkening sky still lingered on the portraits of the Hurly family.

'Doubtless he is like this,' said the squire, pointing to a fair-haired young man with a mild face, a brother of his own who had been lost at sea.

But Lisa shook her head, and went softly on tiptoe from one picture to another, peering into the canvas, and still turning away troubled. But at last a shriek of delight startled the shadowy chamber.

'Ah, here he is! See, here he is, the noble signor, the beautiful signor, not half so handsome as he looked five days ago, when talking to poor little Lisa! Dear sir and madam, you are now content. Now take me to the organ, that I may commence to do his bidding at once.'

The mistress of Hurly Burly clung fast by her husband's arm.

'How old are you, girl?' she said faintly.

'Eighteen,' said the visitor impatiently, moving towards the door.

'And my son has been dead for twenty years!' said his mother, and swooned on her husband's breast.

'Order the carriage at once,' said Mistress Hurly, recovering from her swoon; 'I will take her to Margaret Calderwood. Margaret will tell her the story. Margaret will bring her to reason. No, not to-morrow; I cannot bear to-morrow, it is so far away. We must go to-night.'

The little signora thought the old lady mad, but she put on her cloak again obediently, and took her seat beside Mistress Hurly in the Hurly family coach. The moon that looked in at them through the pane as they lumbered along was not whiter than the aged face of the squire's wife, whose dim faded eyes were fixed upon it in doubt and awe too great for tears or words. Lisa, too, from her corner gloated upon the moon, her black eyes shining with passionate dreams.

A carriage rolled away from the Calderwood door as the Hurly coach drew up at the steps. Margaret Calderwood had just returned from a dinner-party, and at the open door a splendid figure was standing, a tall woman dressed in brown velvet, the diamonds on her bosom glistening in the moonlight that revealed her, pouring, as it did, over the house from eaves to basement. Mistress Hurly fell into her outstretched arms with a groan, and the strong woman carried her aged friend, like a baby, into the house. Little Lisa was overlooked, and sat down contentedly on the threshold to gloat awhile longer on the moon, and to thrum imaginary sonatas on the doorstep.

There were tears and sobs in the dusk, moonlit room into which Margaret Calderwood carried her friend. There was a long consultation, and then Margaret, having hushed away the grieving woman into some quiet corner, came forth to look for the little dark-faced stranger, who had arrived, so unwelcome, from beyond the seas, with such wild communication from the dead.

Up the grand staircase of handsome Calderwood the little woman followed the tall one into a large chamber where a lamp burned, showing Lisa, if she cared to see it, that this mansion of Calderwood was fitted with much greater luxury and richness than was that of Hurly Burly. The appointments of this room announced it the sanctum of a woman who depended for the interest of her life upon resources of intellect and taste. Lisa noticed nothing but a morsel of biscuit that was lying on a plate.

'May I have it?' said she eagerly. 'It is so long since I have eaten. I am hungry.'

Margaret Calderwood gazed at her with a sorrowful, motherly look, and, parting the fringing hair on her forehead, kissed her. Lisa, staring at her in wonder, returned the caress with ardour. Margaret's large fair shoulders, Madonna face, and yellow braided hair, excited a rapture within her. But when food was brought her, she flew to it and ate.

'It is better than I have ever eaten at home!' she said gratefully. And Margaret Calderwood murmured, 'She is physically healthy, at least.'

'And now, Lisa,' said Margaret Calderwood, 'come and

tell me the whole history of the grand signor who sent you to England to play the organ.'

Then Lisa crept in behind a chair, and her eyes began to burn and her fingers to thrum, and she repeated word for word her story as she had told it at Hurly Burly.

When she had finished, Margaret Calderwood began to pace up and down the floor with a very troubled face. Lisa watched her, fascinated, and, when she bade her listen to a story which she would relate to her, folded her restless hands together meekly, and listened.

'Twenty years ago, Lisa, Mr. and Mrs. Hurly had a son. He was handsome, like that portrait you saw in the gallery, and he had brilliant talents. He was idolized by his father and mother, and all who knew him felt obliged to love him. I was then a happy girl of twenty. I was an orphan, and Mrs. Hurly, who had been my mother's friend, was like a mother to me. I, too, was petted and caressed by all my friends, and I was very wealthy; but I only valued admiration, riches – every good gift that fell to my share – just in proportion as they seemed of worth in the eyes of Lewis Hurly. I was his affianced wife, and I loved him well.

'All the fondness and pride that were lavished on him could not keep him from falling into evil ways, nor from becoming rapidly more and more abandoned to wickedness, till even those who loved him best despaired of seeing his reformation. I prayed him with tears, for my sake, if not for that of his grieving mother, to save himself before it was too late. But to my horror I found that my power was gone, my words did not even move him; he loved me no more. I tried to think that this was some fit of madness that would pass, and still clung to hope. At last his own mother forbade me to see him.'

Here Margaret Calderwood paused, seemingly in bitter thought, but resumed:

'He and a party of his boon companions, named by themselves the "Devil's Club", were in the habit of practising all kinds of unholy pranks in the country. They had midnight carousings on the tombstones in the village graveyard; they carried away helpless old men and children, whom they tortured by making believe to bury them alive; they raised the dead and placed them sitting round the tombstones at a mock feast. On one occasion there was a very sad funeral from the village. The corpse was carried into the church, and prayers were read over the coffin, the chief mourner, the aged father of the dead man, standing weeping by. In the midst of this solemn scene the organ suddenly pealed forth a profane tune, and a number of voices shouted a drinking chorus. A groan of execration burst from the crowd, the clergyman turned pale and closed his book, and the old man, the father of the dead, climbed the altar steps, and, raising his arms above his head, uttered a terrible curse. He cursed Lewis Hurly to all eternity, he cursed the organ he played, that it might be dumb henceforth, except under the fingers that had now profaned it, which, he prayed, might be forced to labour upon it till they stiffened in death. And the curse seemed to work, for the organ stood dumb in the church from that day, except when touched by Lewis Hurly.

'For a bravado he had the organ taken down and conveyed to his father's house, where he had it put up in the chamber where it now stands. It was also for a bravado that he played on it every day. But, by-and-by, the amount of time which he spent at it daily began to increase rapidly. We wondered long at this whim, as we called it, and his poor mother thanked God that he had set his heart upon an occupation which would keep him out of harm's way. I was the first to suspect that it was not his own will that kept him hammering at the organ so many laborious hours, while his boon companions tried vainly to draw him away. He used to lock himself up in the room with the organ, but one day I hid myself among the curtains, and saw him writhing on his seat, and heard him groaning as he strove to wrench his hands from the keys, to which they flew back like a needle to a magnet. It was soon plainly to be seen that he was an involuntary slave to the organ; but whether through a madness that had grown within himself, or by some supernatural doom, having its cause in the old man's curse, we did not dare to say. By-and-by there came a time when we were wakened out of our sleep at nights by the rolling of the organ. He wrought now night and day. Food and rest were denied him. His face got haggard, his beard grew long, his eyes started from their sockets. His body became wasted, and his cramped fingers like the claws of a bird. He groaned piteously as he stooped over his cruel toil. All save his mother and I were afraid to go near him. She, poor, tender woman, tried to put wine and food between his lips, while the tortured fingers crawled over the keys; but he only gnashed his teeth at her with curses, and she retreated from him in terror, to pray. At last, one dreadful hour, we found him a ghastly corpse on the ground before the organ.

'From that hour the organ was dumb to the touch of all human fingers. Many, unwilling to believe the story, made persevering endeavours to draw sound from it, in vain. But when the darkened empty room was locked up and left, we heard as loud as ever the well-known sounds humming and rolling through the walls. Night and day the tones of the organ boomed on as before. It seemed that the doom of the wretched man was not yet fulfilled, although his tortured body had been worn out in the terrible struggle to accomplish it. Even his own mother was afraid to go near the room then. So the time went on, and the curse of this perpetual music was not removed from the house. Servants refused to stay about the place. Visitors shunned it. The squire and his wife left their home for years, and returned; left it, and returned again, to find their ears still tortured and their hearts wrung by the unceasing persecution of terrible sounds. At last, but a few months ago, a holy man was found, who locked himself up in the cursed chamber for many days, praying and wrestling with the demon. After he came forth and went away the sounds ceased, and the organ was heard no more. Since then there has been peace in the house. And now, Lisa, your strange appearance and your strange story convince us that you are a victim of a ruse of the Evil One. Be warned in time, and place yourself under the protection of God, that you may be saved from the fearful influences that are at work upon you. Come—'

Margaret Calderwood turned to the corner where the stranger sat, as she had supposed, listening intently. Little Lisa was fast asleep, her hands spread before her as if she played an organ in her dream.

Margaret took the soft brown face to her motherly breast, and kissed the swelling temples, too big with wonder and fancy.

'We will save you from a horrible fate!' she murmured, and carried the girl to bed.

In the morning Lisa was gone. Margaret Calderwood, coming early from her own chamber, went into the girl's room and found the bed empty.

'She is just such a wild thing,' thought Margaret, 'as would rush out at sunrise to hear the larks!' and she went forth to look for her in the meadows, behind the beech hedges, and in the home park. Mistress Hurly, from the breakfast-room window, saw Margaret Calderwood, large and fair in her white morning gown, coming down the garden-path between the rose bushes, with her fresh draperies dabbled by the dew, and a look of trouble on her calm face. Her quest had been unsuccessful. The little foreigner had vanished.

A second search after breakfast proved also fruitless, and towards evening the two women drove back to Hurly Burly together. There all was panic and distress. The squire sat in his study with the doors shut, and his hands over his ears. The servants, with pale faces, were huddled together in whispering groups. The haunted organ was pealing through the house as of old.

Margaret Calderwood hastened to the fatal chamber, and there, sure enough, was Lisa, perched upon the high seat before the organ, beating the keys with her small hands, her slight figure swaying, and the evening sunshine playing about her weird head. Sweet unearthly music she wrung from the groaning heart of the organ – wild melodies, mounting to rapturous heights and falling to mournful depths. She wandered from Mendelssohn to Mozart, and from Mozart to Beethoven. Margaret stood fascinated awhile by the ravishing beauty of the sounds she heard, but, rousing herself quickly, put her arms round the musician and forced her away from the chamber. Lisa returned next day, however, and was not so easily coaxed from her post again. Day after day she laboured at the organ, growing paler and thinner and more weird-looking as time went on.

'I work so hard,' she said to Mrs. Hurly. 'The signor, your son, is he pleased? Ask him to come and tell me himself if he is pleased.'

Mistress Hurly got ill and took to her bed. The squire swore at the young foreign baggage, and roamed abroad. Margaret Calderwood was the only one who stood by to watch the fate of the little organist. The curse of the organ was upon Lisa; it spoke under her hand, and her hand was its slave.

At last she announced rapturously that she had had a visit from the brave signor, who had commended her industry, and urged her to work yet harder. After that she ceased to hold any communication with the living. Time after time Margaret Calderwood wrapped her arms about the frail thing, and carried her away by force, locking the door of the fatal chamber. But locking the chamber and burying the key were of no avail. The door stood open again, and Lisa was labouring on her perch.

One night, wakened from her sleep by the well-known humming and moaning of the organ, Margaret dressed hurriedly and hastened to the unholy room. Moonlight was pouring down the staircase and passages of Hurly Burly. It shone on the marble bust of the dead Lewis Hurly, that stood in the niche above his mother's sitting-room door. The organ room was full of it when Margaret pushed open the door and entered – full of the pale green moonlight from the window, mingled with another light, a dull lurid glare which seemed to centre round a dark shadow, like the figure of a man standing by the organ, and throwing out in fantastic relief the slight form of Lisa writhing, rather than swaying, back and forward, as if in agony. The sounds that came from the organ were broken and meaningless, as if the hands of the player lagged and stumbled on the keys. Between the intermittent chords low moaning cries broke from Lisa, and the dark figure bent towards her with menacing gestures. Trembling with the sickness of supernatural fear, yet strong of will, Margaret Calderwood crept forward within the lurid light, and was drawn into its influence. It grew and intensified upon her, it dazzled and blinded her at first; but presently, by a daring effort of will, she raised her eyes, and beheld Lisa's face convulsed with torture in the burning glare, and bending over her the figure and the features of Lewis Hurly! Smitten with horror, Margaret did not even then lose her presence of mind. She wound her strong arms around the wretched girl and dragged her from her seat and out of the influence of the lurid light, which immediately paled away and vanished. She carried her to her own bed, where Lisa lay, a wasted wreck, raving about the cruelty of the pitiless signor who would not see that she was labouring her best. Her poor cramped hands kept beating the coverlet, as though she were still at her agonizing task.

Margaret Calderwood bathed her burning temples, and placed fresh flowers upon her pillow. She opened the blinds and windows, and let in the sweet morning air and sunshine and then, looking up at the newly awakened sky with its fair promise of hope for the day, and down at the dewy fields, and afar off at the dark green woods with the purple mists still hovering about them, she prayed that a way might be shown her by which to put an end to this curse. She prayed for Lisa, and then, thinking that the girl rested somewhat, stole from the room. She thought that she had locked the door behind her.

She went downstairs with a pale, resolved face, and, without consulting anyone, sent to the village for a bricklayer. Afterwards she sat by Mistress Hurly's bedside, and explained to her what was to be done. Presently she went to the door of Lisa's room, and hearing no sound, thought the girl slept, and stole away. By-and-by she went downstairs, and found that the bricklayer had arrived and already begun his task of building up the organ-room door. He was a swift workman, and the chamber was soon sealed safely with stone and mortar.

Having seen this work finished, Margaret Calderwood went and listened again at Lisa's door; and still hearing no sound, she returned, and took her seat at Mrs. Hurly's bedside once more. It was towards evening that she at last entered her room to assure herself of the comfort of Lisa's sleep. But the bed and room were empty. Lisa had disappeared.

Then the search began, upstairs and downstairs, in the garden, in the grounds, in the fields and meadows. No Lisa. Margaret Calderwood ordered the carriage and drove to Calderwood to see if the strange little Will-o'-the-wisp might have made her way there; then to the village, and to many other places in the neighbourhood which it was not possible she could have reached. She made inquiries everywhere; she pondered and puzzled over the matter. In the weak, suffering state that the girl was in, how far could she have crawled?

After two days' search, Margaret returned to Hurly Burly. She was sad and tired, and the evening was chill. She sat over the fire wrapped in her shawl when little Bess came to her, weeping behind her muslin apron.

'If you'd speak to Mistress Hurly about it, please, ma'am,' she said. 'I love her dearly, and it breaks my heart to go away, but the organ haven't done yet, ma'am, and I'm frightened out of my life, so I can't stay.'

'Who has heard the organ, and when?' asked Margaret Calderwood, rising to her feet.

'Please, ma'am, I heard it the night you went away – the night after the door was built up!'

'And not since?'

'No, ma'am,' hesitatingly, 'not since. Hist! hark, ma'am! Is not that like the sound of it now?'

'No,' said Margaret Calderwood; 'it is only the wind.' But pale as death she flew down the stairs and laid her ear to the yet damp mortar of the newly-built wall. All was silent. There was no sound but the monotonous sough of the wind in the trees outside. Then Margaret began to dash her soft shoulder against the strong wall, and to pick the mortar away with her white fingers, and to cry out for the bricklayer who had built up the door.

It was midnight, but the bricklayer left his bed in the village, and obeyed the summons to Hurly Burly. The pale woman stood by and watched him undo all his work of three days ago, and the servants gathered about in trembling groups, wondering what was to happen next.

What happened next was this: When an opening was made the man entered the room with a light, Margaret Calderwood and others following. A heap of something dark was lying on the ground at the foot of the organ. Many groans arose in the fatal chamber. Here was little Lisa dead!

When Mistress Hurly was able to move, the squire and his wife went to live in France, where they remained till their death. Hurly Burly was shut up and deserted for many years. Lately it has passed into new hands. The organ has been taken down and banished, and the room is a bed-chamber, more luxuriously furnished than any in the house. But no one sleeps in it twice.

Margaret Calderwood was carried to her grave the other day a very aged woman.

THE BECKONING HAND

by Grant Allen

A native of Kingston, Canada, Charles Grant Allen (1848–1899) was educated in France and England. Settling in England he found his chosen career of teacher complicated by ill health and the responsibility of an invalid wife. Seeking a pleasanter climate, he became for a time Professor of 'Mental and Moral Philosophy' at the ambitious University for Negroes in Spanish Town, Jamaica. This enterprising project collapsed and, in 1876, Allen returned to England determined to become a successful writer.

His fiction, sometimes written under the name Cecil Power, proved popular but he was also acclaimed for an astonishing diversity of factual works. He wrote Physiological Aesthetics (1877) *and* Anglo Saxon Britain (1881) *and wrote with equal ease and authority about scientific subjects, plant-life, evolution and the artistic treasures of Europe. His studies of evolutionary theory drew praise from Darwin and Huxley.*

Allen's experiences in the West Indies probably inspired this memorable tale of Voodoo.

I

I FIRST met Césarine Vivian in the stalls at the Ambiguities Theatre.

I had promised to take Mrs. Latham and Irene to see the French plays which were then being acted by Marie Leroux's celebrated Palais Royal company. I wasn't at the time exactly engaged to poor Irene: it has always been a comfort to me that I wasn't engaged to her, though I knew Irene herself considered it practically equivalent to an understood engagement. We had known one another intimately from childhood upward, for the Lathams were a sort of second cousins of ours, three times removed: and we had always called one another by our Christian names, and been very fond of one another in a simple girlish and boyish fashion as long as we could either of us remember. Still, I maintain, there was no definite understanding between us; and if Mrs. Latham thought I had been paying Irene attentions, she must have known that a young man of two and twenty, with a decent fortune and a nice estate down in Devonshire, was likely to look about him for a while before he thought of settling down and marrying quietly.

I had brought the yacht up to London Bridge, and was living on board in picnic style, and running about town casually, when I took Irene and her mother to see 'Faustine,' at the Ambiguities. As soon as we had got in and taken our places, Irene whispered to me, touching my hand lightly with her fan, 'Just look at the very dark girl on the other side of you, Harry! Did you ever in your life see anybody so perfectly beautiful?'

It has alas been a great comfort to me, too, that Irene

herself was the first person to call my attention to Césarine Vivian's extraordinary beauty.

I turned round, as if by accident, and gave a passing glance, where Irene waved her fan, at the girl beside me. She was beautiful, certainly, in a terrible, grand, statuesque style of beauty; and I saw at a glimpse that she had Southern blood in her veins, perhaps Negro, perhaps Moorish, perhaps only Spanish, or Italian, or Provençal. Her features were proud and somewhat Jewish-looking; her eyes large, dark and haughty; her black hair waved slightly in sinuous undulations as it passed across her high, broad forehead; her complexion, though a dusky olive in tone, was clear and rich, and daintily transparent; and her lips were thin and very slightly curled at the delicate corners, with a peculiarly imperious and almost scornful expression of fixed disdain. I had never before beheld anywhere such a magnificently repellent specimen of womanhood. For a second or so, as I looked her eyes met mine with a defiant inquiry, and I was conscious that moment of some strange and weird fascination in her glance that seemed to draw me irresistibly towards her, at the same time that I hardly dared to fix my gaze steadily upon the piercing eyes that looked through and through me with their keen penetration.

'She's very beautiful, no doubt,' I whispered back to Irene in a low undertone, 'though I must confess I don't exactly like the look of her. She's a trifle too much of a tragedy queen for my taste: a Lady Macbeth, or a Beatrice Cenci, or a Clytemnestra. I prefer our simple little English prettiness to this southern splendour. It's more to our English liking than these tall and stately Italian enchantresses. Besides, I fancy the girl looks as if she had a drop or two of black blood somewhere about her.'

'Oh, no,' Irene cried warmly. 'Impossible, Harry. She's exquisite: exquisite. Italian, you know, or something of that sort. Italian girls have always got that peculiar gipsy-like type of beauty.'

Low as we spoke, the girl seemed to know by instinct we were talking about her; for she drew away the ends of her light wrap coldly, in a significant fashion, and turned with her opera-glass in the opposite direction, as if on purpose to avoid looking towards us.

A minute later the curtain rose, and the first act of Halévy's 'Faustine' distracted my attention for the moment from the beautiful stranger.

Marie Leroux took the part of the great empress. She was grand, stately, imposing, no doubt, but somehow it seemed to me she didn't come up quite so well as usual that evening to one's ideal picture of the terrible, audacious, superb Roman woman. I leant over and murmured so to Irene. 'Don't you know why?' Irene whispered back to me with a faint movement of the play-bill towards the beautiful stranger.

'No,' I answered; 'I haven't really the slightest conception.'

'Why,' she whispered, smiling; 'just look beside you. Could anybody bear comparison for a moment as a Faustine with that splendid creature in the stall next to you?'

I stole a glance sideways as she spoke. It was quite true. The girl by my side was the real Faustine, the exact embodiment of the dramatist's creation; and Marie Leroux, with her stagey effects and her actress's pretences, could not in any way stand the contrast with the genuine empress who sat there eagerly watching her.

The girl saw me glance quickly from her towards the actress and from the actress back to her, and shrank aside, not with coquettish timidity, but half angrily and half as if flattered and pleased at the implied compliment. 'Papa,' she said to the very English-looking gentleman who sat beyond her, 'ce monsieur-ci . . .' I couldn't catch the end of the sentence.

She was French, then, not Italian or Spanish; yet a more perfect Englishman than the man she called 'papa' it would be difficult to discover on a long summer's day in all London.

'My dear,' her father whispered back in English, 'if I were you . . .' and the rest of that sentence also was quite inaudible to me.

My interest was now fully roused in the beautiful stranger, who sat evidently with her father and sister, and drank in every word of the play as it proceeded with the intensest interest. As for me, I hardly cared to look at the actors, so absorbed was I in my queenly neighbour. I made a bare pretence of watching the stage every five minutes, and saying a few words now and again to Irene or her mother; but my real attention was all the time furtively directed to the girl beside me. Not that I was taken with her, quite the contrary; she distinctly repelled me; but she seemed to exercise over me for all that the same strange and indescribable fascination which is often possessed by some horrible sight that you would give worlds to avoid, and yet cannot for your life help intently gazing upon.

Between the third and fourth acts Irene whispered to me again, 'I can't keep my eyes off her, Harry. She's wonderfully beautiful. Confess now: aren't you over head and ears in love with her?'

I looked at Irene's sweet little peaceful English face, and I answered truthfully, 'No, Irene. If I wanted to fall in love, I should find somebody—'

'Nonsense, Harry,' Irene cried, blushing a little, and holding up her fan before her nervously. 'She's a thousand times prettier and handsomer in every way—'

'Prettier?'

'Than I am.'

At that moment the curtain rose, and Marie Leroux came forward once more with her imperial diadem, in the very act of defying and bearding the enraged emperor.

It was a great scene. The whole theatre hung upon her words for twenty minutes. The effect was sublime. Even I myself felt my interest aroused at last in the consummate spectacle. I glanced round to observe my neighbour. She sat there, straining her gaze upon the stage, and heaving her bosom with suppressed emotion. In a second, the spell was broken again. Beside that tall, dark southern girl in her queenly beauty, with her flashing eyes and quivering nostrils, intensely moved by the passion of the play, the mere actress who mouthed and gesticulated before us by the footlights was as sounding brass and a tinkling cymbal. My companion in the stalls was the genuine Faustine: the player on the stage was but a false pretender.

As I looked a cry arose from the wings: a hushed cry at first, a buzz or hum; rising louder and ever louder still, as a red glare burst upon the scene from the background. Then a voice from the side boxes rang out suddenly above the confused murmur and the ranting of the actors – 'Fire! Fire!'

Almost before I knew what had happened, the mob in the stalls, like the mob in the gallery, was surging and swaying wildly towards the exits, in a general struggle for life of the fierce old selfish barbaric pattern. Dense clouds of smoke rolled from the stage and filled the length and breadth of the auditorium; tongues of flame licked up the pasteboard scenes and hangings, like so much paper; women screamed, and fought, and fainted; men pushed one another aside and hustled and elbowed, in one wild effort to make for the doors at all hazards to the lives of their neighbours. Never before had I so vividly realized how near the savage lies to the surface in our best and highest civilized society. I had to realize it still more vividly and more terribly afterwards.

One person alone I observed calm and erect, resisting quietly all pushes and thrusts, and moving with slow deliberateness to the door, as if wholly unconcerned at the universal noise and hubbub and tumult around her. It was the dark girl from the stalls beside me.

For myself, my one thought of course was for poor Irene and Mrs. Latham. Fortunately, I am a strong and well-built man, and by keeping the two women in front of me, and thrusting hard with my elbows on either side to keep off the crush, I managed to make a tolerably clear road for them down the central row of stalls and out on to the big external staircase. The dark girl, now separated from her father and sister by the rush, was close in front of me. By a careful side movement, I managed to include her also in our party. She looked up to me gratefully with her big eyes, and her mouth broke into a charming smile as she turned and said in perfect English, 'I am much obliged to you for your kind assistance.' Irene's cheek was pale as death; but through the strange young lady's olive skin the bright blood still burned and glowed amid that frantic panic as calmly as ever.

We had reached the bottom of the steps, and were out into the front, when suddenly the strange lady turned around and gave a little cry of disappointment. 'Mes lorgnettes! Mes lorgnettes!' she said. Then glancing round carelessly to me she went on in English: 'I have left my opera-glasses inside on the vacant seat. I think, if you will excuse me, I'll go back and fetch them.'

'It's impossible,' I cried, 'my dear madam. Utterly impossible They'll crush you underfoot. They'll tear you to pieces.'

She smiled a strange haughty smile, as if amused at the idea, but merely answered, 'I think not,' and tried to pass lightly by me.

I held her arm. I didn't know then she was as strong as I was. 'Don't go,' I said imploringly. 'They will certainly kill you. It would be impossible to stem a mob like this one.'

She smiled again, and darted back in silence before I could stop her.

Irene and Mrs. Latham were now fairly out of all danger. 'Go on, Irene,' I said loosing her arm. 'Policeman, get these ladies safely out. I must go back and take care of that mad woman.'

'Go, go quick,' Irene cried. 'If you don't go, she'll be killed, Harry.'

I rushed back wildly after her, battling as well as I was able against the frantic rush of panic-stricken fugitives, and found my companion struggling still upon the main staircase. I helped her to make her way back into the burning theatre, and she ran lightly through the dense smoke to the stall she had occupied, and took the opera-glasses from the vacant place. Then she turned to me once more with a smile of triumph. 'People lose their heads so,' she said, 'in all these crushes. I came back on purpose to show papa I wasn't going to be frightened into leaving my opera-glasses. I should have been eternally ashamed of myself if I had come away and left them in the theatre.'

'Quick,' I answered, gasping for breath. 'If you don't make haste, we shall be choked to death, or the roof itself will fall in upon us and crush us!'

She looked up where I pointed with a hasty glance, and then made her way back again quickly to the staircase. As we hurried out, the timbers of the stage were beginning to fall in, and the engines were already playing fiercely upon the raging flames. I took her hand and almost dragged her out into the open. When we reached the Strand, we were both wet through, and terribly blackened with smoke and ashes. Pushing our way through the dense crowd, I called a hansom. She jumped in lightly. 'Thank you so much,' she said, quite carelessly. 'Will you kindly tell him where to drive? Twenty-seven, Seymour Crescent.'

'I'll see you home, if you'll allow me,' I answered, 'Under these circumstances, I trust I may be permitted.'

'As you like,' she said, smiling enchantingly. 'You are very good. My name is Césarine Vivian. Papa will be very much obliged to you for your kind assistance.'

I drove round to the Lathams' after dropping Miss Vivian at her father's door, to assure myelf of Irene's safety, and to let them know of my own return unhurt from my perilous adventure. Irene met me on the doorstep, pale as death still. 'Thank heaven,' she cried, 'Harry, you're safe back again! And that poor girl? What has become of her?'

'I left her,' I said, 'at Seymour Crescent.'

Irene burst into a flood of tears. 'Oh, Harry,' she cried, 'I thought she would have been killed there. It was brave of you, indeed, to help her through with it.'

II

Next day, Mr. Vivian called on me at the Oxford and Cambridge, the address on the card I had given his daughter. I was in the club when he called, and I found him a pleasant, good-natured Cornishman, with very little that was strange or romantic in any way about him. He thanked me heartily, but not too effusively, for the care I had taken of Miss Vivian over-night; and he was not so overcome with parental emotion as not to smoke a very good Havana, or to refuse my offer of a brandy and seltzer. We got on very well together, and I soon gathered from what my new acquaintance said that, though he belonged to one of the best families in Cornwall, he had been an English merchant in Haiti, and had made his money chiefly in the coffee trade. He was a widower, I learned incidentally, and his daughters had been brought up for some years in England, though at their mother's request they had also passed part of their lives in convent schools in Paris and Rouen. 'Mrs. Vivian was a Haitian, you know,' he said casually: 'Catholic of course. The girls are Catholics. They're good girls, though they're my own daughters; and Césarine, your friend of last night, is supposed to be clever. I'm no judge myself: I don't know about it. Oh, by the way, Césarine said she hadn't thanked you half enough herself yesterday, and I was to be sure and bring you round this afternoon to a cup of tea with us at Seymour Crescent.'

In spite of the impression Mdlle Césarine had made upon me the night before, I somehow didn't feel at all desirous of meeting her again. I was impressed, it is true, but not favourably. There seemed to me something uncanny and weird about her which made me shrink from seeing anything more of her if I could possibly avoid it. And as it happened, I was luckily engaged that very afternoon to tea at Irene's. I made the excuse, and added somewhat pointedly – on purpose that it might be repeated to Mdlle Césarine – 'Miss Latham is a very old and particular friend of mine – a friend whom I couldn't for worlds think of disappointing.'

Mr. Vivian laughed the matter off. 'I shall catch it from Césarine,' he said good-humouredly, 'for not bringing her cavalier to receive her formal thanks in person. Our West-Indian born girls, you know, are very imperious. But if you can't, you can't, of course, so there's an end of it, and it's no use talking any more about it.'

I can't say why, but at that moment, in spite of my intense desire not to meet Césarine again, I felt I would have given whole worlds if he would have pressed me to come in spite of myself. But, as it happened, he didn't.

At five o'clock, I drove round in a hansom as arranged, to Irene's, having almost made up my mind, if I found her alone, to come to a definite understanding with her and call it an engagement. She wasn't alone, however. As I entered the drawing-room, I saw a tall and graceful lady sitting opposite her, holding a cup of tea, and with her back towards me. The lady rose, moved round, and bowed. To my immense surprise, I found it was Césarine.

I noted to myself at the moment, too, that in my heart, though I had seen her but once before, I thought of her already simply as Césarine. And I was pleased to see her: fascinated: spell-bound.

Césarine smiled at my evident surprise. 'Papa and I met Miss Latham this afternoon in Bond Street,' she said gaily, in answer to my mute inquiry, 'and we stopped and spoke to one another, of course, about last night; and papa said you couldn't come round to tea with us in the Crescent, because you were engaged already to Miss Latham. And Miss Latham very kindly asked me to drive over and take tea with her, as I was so anxious to thank you once more for your great kindness to me yesterday.'

'And Miss Vivian was good enough to waive all ceremony,' Irene put in, 'and come round to us as you see, without further introduction.'

I stopped and talked all the time I was there to Irene; but, somehow, whatever I said, Césarine managed to intercept it, and I caught myself quite guiltily looking at her from time to time, with an inexpressible attraction that I could not account for.

By-and-by, Mr. Vivian's carriage called for Césarine, and I was left a few minutes alone with Irene.

'Well, what do you think of her?' Irene asked me simply.

I turned my eyes away: I dared not meet hers. 'I think she's very handsome,' I replied evasively.

'Handsome! I should think so. She's wonderful. She's splendid. And doesn't she talk magnificently, too, Harry?'

'She's clever, certainly,' I answered shuffling. 'But I don't know why, I mistrust her, Irene.'

I rose and stood by the door with my hat in my hand, hesitating and trembling. I felt as if I had something to say to Irene, and yet I was half afraid to venture upon saying it. My fingers quivered, a thing very unusual with me. At last I came closer to her, after a long pause, and said, 'Irene.'

Irene started, and the colour flushed suddenly into her cheeks. 'Yes, Harry,' she answered tremulously.

I don't know why, but I couldn't utter it. It was but to say 'I love you,' yet I hadn't the courage. I stood there like a fool, looking at her irresolutely, and then—

The door opened suddenly, and Mrs. Latham entered and interrupted us.

III

I didn't speak again to Irene. The reason was that three days later I received a little note of invitation to lunch at Seymour Crescent from Césarine Vivian.

I didn't want to accept it, and yet I didn't know how to help myself. I went, determined beforehand as soon as ever lunch was over to take away the yacht to the Scotch islands, and leave Césarine and all her enchantments for ever behind me. I was afraid of her, that's the fact, positively afraid of her. I couldn't look her in the face without feeling at once that she exerted a terrible influence over me.

The lunch went off quietly enough, however. We talked about Haiti and the West Indies; about the beautiful foliage and the lovely flowers; about the moonlight nights and the tropical sunsets; and Césarine grew quite enthusiastic over them all. 'You should take your yacht out there some day, Mr. Tristram,' she said softly. 'There is no place on earth so wild and glorious as our own beautiful neglected Haiti.'

She lifted her eyes full upon me as she spoke. I stammered out, like one spellbound, 'I must certainly go, on your recommendation, Mademoiselle Césarine.'

'Why Mademoiselle?' she asked quickly. Then, perceiving I misunderstood her by the start I gave, she added with a blush, 'I mean, why not "Miss Vivian" in plain English?'

'Because you aren't English,' I said confusedly. 'You're Haitian, in reality. Nobody could ever for a moment take you for a mere Englishwoman.'

I meant it for a compliment, but Césarine frowned. I saw I had hurt her, and why; but I did not apologize. Yet I was conscious of having done something very wrong, and I knew I must try my best at once to regain my lost favour with her.

'You will take some coffee after lunch?' Césarine said, as the dishes were removed.

'Oh, certainly, my dear,' her father put in. 'You must show Mr. Tristram how we make coffee in the West Indian fashion.'

Césarine smiled, and poured it out – black coffee, very strong, and into each cup she poured a little glass of excellent pale neat cognac. It seemed to me that she poured the cognac like a conjuror's trick; but everything about her was so strange and lurid that I took very little notice of the matter at that particular moment. It certainly was delicious coffee: I never tasted anything like it.

After lunch, we went into the drawing-room, and thence Césarine took me alone into the pretty conservatory. She wanted to show me some of her beautiful Haitian orchids, she said; she had brought the orchids herself years ago from Haiti. How long we stood there I could never tell. I seemed as if intoxicated with her presence. I had forgotten now all about my distrust of her: I had forgotten all about Irene and what I wished to say to her: I was conscious only of Césarine's great dark eyes, looking through and through me with their piercing glance, and Césarine's figure, tall and stately, but very voluptuous, standing close beside me, and heaving regularly as we looked at the orchids. She talked to me in a low and dreamy voice; and whether the Château Larose at lunch had got into my head, or whatever it might be, I felt only dimly and faintly aware of what was passing around me. I was unmanned with love, I suppose: but, however it may have been, I certainly moved and spoke that afternoon like a man in a trance from which he cannot by any effort of his own possibly awake himself.

'Yes, yes,' I overheard Césarine saying at last, as through a mist of emotion, 'you must go some day and see our beautiful mountainous Haiti. I must go myself. I long to go again. I don't care for this gloomy, dull, sunless England. A hand seems always to be beckoning me there. I shall obey it some day, for Haiti – our lovely Haiti, is too beautiful.'

Her voice was low and marvellously musical. 'Mademoiselle Césarine,' I began timidly.

She pouted and looked at me. 'Mademoiselle again,' she said in a pettish way. 'I told you not to call me so, didn't I?'

'Well, then, Césarine,' I went on boldly. She laughed low, a little laugh of triumph, but did not correct or check me in any way.

'Césarine,' I continued, lingering I know not why over the syllables of the name, 'I will go, as you say. I shall see Haiti. Why should we not both go together?'

She looked up at me eagerly with a sudden look of hushed inquiry. 'You mean it?' she asked, trembling visibly. 'You mean it, Mr. Tristram? You know what you are saying?'

'Césarine,' I answered, 'I mean it. I know it. I cannot go

away from you and leave you. Something seems to tie me. I am not my own master.... Césarine, I love you.'

My head whirled as I said the words, but I meant them at the time, and heaven knows I tried ever after to live up to them.

She clutched my arm convulsively for a moment. Her face was aglow with a wonderful light, and her eyes burned like a pair of diamonds. 'But the other girl!' she cried. 'Her! Miss Latham! The one you call Irene! You are ... in love with her! Are you not? Tell me!'

'I have never proposed to Irene,' I replied slowly. 'I have never asked any other woman but you to marry me, Césarine.'

She answered me nothing, but my face was very near hers, and I bent forward and kissed her suddenly. To my immense surprise, instead of struggling or drawing away, she kissed me back a fervent kiss, with lips hard pressed to mine, and the tears trickled slowly down her cheeks in a strange fashion. 'You are mine,' she cried. 'Mine for ever. I have won you. She shall not have you. I knew you were mine the moment I looked upon you. The hand beckoned me. I knew I should get you.'

'Come up into my den, Mr. Tristam, and have a smoke,' my host interrupted in his bluff voice, putting his head in unexpectedly at the conservatory door. 'I think I can offer you a capital Manilla.'

The sound woke me as if from some terrible dream, and I followed him still in a sort of stupor up to the smoking room.

IV

That very evening I went to see Irene. My brain was whirling even yet, and I hardly knew what I was doing; but the cool air revived me a little, and by the time I reached the Lathams' I almost felt myself again.

Irene came down to the drawing-room to see me alone. I saw what she expected, and the shame of my duplicity overcame me utterly.

I took both her hands in mine and stood opposite her, ashamed to look her in the face, and with the terrible confession weighing me down like a burden of guilt. 'Irene,' I blurted out, without preface or comment, 'I have just proposed to Césarine Vivian.'

Irene drew back a moment and took a long breath. Then she said, with a tremor in her voice, but without a tear or a cry, 'I expected it, Harry. I thought you meant it. I saw you were terribly, horribly in love with her.'

'Irene,' I cried, passionately and remorsefully flinging myself upon the sofa in an agony of repentance, 'I do not love her. I have never cared for her. I'm afraid of her, fascinated by her. I love you, Irene, you and you only. The moment I'm away from her, I hate her, I hate her. For heaven's sake, tell me what am I to do! I do not love her. I hate her, Irene.'

Irene came up to me and soothed my hair tenderly with her hand. 'Don't, Harry,' she said, with sisterly kindliness. 'Don't speak so. Don't give way to it. I know what you feel. I know what you think. But I am not angry with you. You mustn't talk like that. If she has accepted you, you must go and marry her. I have nothing to reproach you with: nothing, nothing. Never say such words to me again. Let us be as we have always been, friends only.'

'Irene,' I cried, lifting up my head and looking at her wildly, 'it is the truth: I do not love her, except when I am with her: and then, some strange enchantment seems to come over me. I don't know what it is, but I can't escape it. In my heart, Irene, in my heart of hearts, I love you, and you only. I can never love her as I love you, Irene. My darling, my darling, tell me how to get myself away from her.'

'Hush,' Irene said, laying her hand on mine persuasively. 'You're excited to-night, Harry. You are flushed and feverish. You don't know what you're saying. You mustn't talk so. If you do, you'll make me hate you and despise you. You must keep your word now, and marry Miss Vivian.'

V

The next six weeks seem to me still like a vague dream: everything happened so hastily and strangely. I got a note next day from Irene. It was very short. 'Dearest Harry, – Mamma and I think, under the circumstances, it would be best for us to leave London for a few weeks. I am not angry with you. With best love, ever yours affectionately, Irene.'

I was wild when I received it. I couldn't bear to part so with Irene. I would find out where they were going and follow them immediately. I would write a note and break off my mad engagement with Césarine. I must have been drunk or insane when I made it. I couldn't imagine what I could have been doing.

On my way round to inquire at the Latham's, a carriage came suddenly upon me at a sharp corner. A lady bowed to me from it. It was Césarine with her father. They pulled up and spoke to me. From that moment my doom was sealed. The old fascination came back at once, and I followed Césarine blindly home to her house to luncheon, her accepted lover.

In six weeks more we were really married.

The first seven or eight months of our married life passed away happily enough. As soon as I was actually married to

Césarine, that strange feeling I had at first experienced about her slowly wore off in the closer, commonplace, daily intercourse of married life. I almost smiled at myself for ever having felt it. Césarine was so beautiful and so queenly a person, that when I took her down home to Devonshire, and introduced her to the old manor, I really found myself immensely proud of her. Everybody at Teignbury was delighted and struck with her; and, what was a great deal more to the point, I began to discover that I was positively in love with her myself, into the bargain. She softened and melted immensely on nearer acquaintance; the Faustina air faded slowly away, when one saw her in her own home among her own occupations; and I came to look on her as a beautiful, simple, innocent girl, delighted with all our country pleasures, fond of a breezy canter on the slopes of Dartmoor, and taking an affectionate interest in the ducks and chickens, which I could hardly ever have conceived even as possible when I first saw her in Seymour Crescent. The imperious, mysterious, terrible Césarine disappeared entirely, and I found in her place, to my immense relief, that I had married a graceful, gentle, tender-hearted English girl, with just a pleasant occasional touch of southern fire and impetuosity.

As winter came round again, however, Césarine's cheeks began to look a little thinner than usual; and she had such a constant, troublesome cough, that I began to be a trifle alarmed at her strange symptoms. Césarine herself laughed off my fears. 'It's nothing, Harry,' she would say; 'nothing at all, I assure you, dear. A few good rides on the moor will set me right again. It's all the result of that horrid London. I'm a country-born girl, and I hate big towns. I never want to live in town again, Harry.'

I called in our best Exeter doctor, and he largely confirmed Césarine's own simple view of the situation.

'There's nothing organically wrong with Mrs. Tristram's constitution,' he said confidently. 'No weakness of the lungs or heart in any way. She has merely run down – outlived her strength a little. A winter in some warm, genial climate would set her up again, I haven't the least hesitation in saying.'

'Let us go to Algeria with the yacht, Reeney,' I suggested much reassured.

'Why Algeria?' Césarine replied, with brightening eyes. 'Oh, Harry, why not dear old Haiti? You said once you would go there with me – you remember when, darling; why not keep your promise now, and go there? I want to go there, Harry: I'm longing to go there.' And she held out her delicately moulded hand in front of her, as if beckoning me, and drawing me on to Haiti after her.

'Ah, yes; why not the West Indies?' the Exeter doctor answered meditatively. 'I think I understood you that Mrs. Tristram is West Indian born. Quite so. Quite so. Her native air. Depend upon it, that's the best place for her. By all means, I should say, try Haiti.'

I don't know why, but the notion for some reason displeased me immensely. There was something about Césarine's eyes, somehow, when she beckoned with her hand in that strange fashion, which reminded me exactly of the weird, uncanny, indescribable impression she had made upon me when I first knew her. Still I was very fond of Césarine, and if she and the doctor were both agreed that Haiti would be the very best place for her, it would be foolish and wrong for me to interfere with their joint wisdom. Depend upon it, a woman often knows what is the matter with her better than any man, even her husband, can possibly tell her.

The end of it all was, that in less than a month from that day, we were out in the yacht on the broad Atlantic, with the cliffs of Falmouth and the Lizard Point fading slowly behind us in the distance; and the white spray dashing in front of us, like fingers beckoning us on to Haiti.

VI

The bay of Port-au-Prince is hot and simmering, a deep basin enclosed in a ringing semicircle of mountains, with scarce a breath blowing on the harbour, and with tall cocoanut palms rising unmoved into the still air above on the low sand-spits that close it in to seaward. The town itself is wretched, squalid, and hopelessly ram-shackled, a despondent collection of tumbledown wooden houses, interspersed with indescribable Negro huts, mere human rabbit-hutches, where parents and children herd together, in one higgledy-piggledy, tropical confusion. I had never in my days seen anything more painfully desolate and dreary, and I feared that Césarine, who had not been here since she was a girl of fourteen, would be somewhat depressed at the horrid actuality, after her exalted fanciful ideals of the remembered Haiti. But, to my immense surprise, as it turned out, Césarine did not appear at all shocked or taken aback at the squalor and wretchedness all around her. On the contrary, the very air of the place seemed to inspire her from the first with fresh vigour; her cough disappeared at once as if by magic; and the colour returned forthwith to her cheeks, almost as soon as we had fairly cast anchor in Haitian waters.

The very first day we arrived at Port-au-Prince, Césarine said to me, with more shyness than I had ever yet seen her exhibit, 'If you wouldn't mind it, Harry, I should like to go at once, this morning – and see my grandmother.'

I started with astonishment. 'Your grandmother,

Césarine!' I cried incredulously. 'My darling! I didn't know you had a grandmother living.'

'Yes, I have,' she answered, with some slight hesitation, 'and I think if you wouldn't object to it, Harry, I'd rather go and see her alone, the first time at least, please dearest.'

In a moment, the obvious truth, which I had always known in a vague sort of fashion, but never thoroughly realized, flashed across my mind in its full vividness, and I merely bowed my head in silence. It was natural she should not wish me to see her meeting with her Haitian grandmother.

She went alone through the streets of Port-au-Prince, without inquiry, like one who knew them familiarly of old, and I dogged her footsteps at a distance unperceived, impelled by the same strange fascination which had so often driven me to follow Césarine wherever she led me. After a few hundred yards, she turned out of the chief business place, and down a tumbledown alley of scattered negro cottages, till she came at last to a rather better house that stood by itself in a little dusty garden of guava-trees and cocoanuts. A rude paling, built negro-wise of broken barrel-staves, nailed rudely together, separated the garden from the compound next to it. I slipped into the compound before Césarine observed me, beckoned the lazy negro from the door of the hut, with one finger placed as a token of silence upon my lips, dropped a dollar into his open palm, and stood behind the paling, looking out into the garden beside me through a hole made by a knot in one of the barrel staves.

Césarine knocked with her hand at the door, and in a moment was answered by an old negress, tall and bony, dressed in a loose sack-like gown of coarse cotton print, with a big red bandanna tied around her short grey hair, and a huge silver cross dangling carelessly upon her bare and wrinkled black neck. She wore no sleeves, and bracelets of strange beads hung loosely around her shrunken and skinny wrists. A more hideous old hag I had never in my life beheld before; and yet I saw, without waiting to observe it, that she had Césarine's great dark eyes and even white teeth, and something of Césarine's figure lingered still in her lithe and sinuous yet erect carriage.

'Grand'mère!' Césarine said convulsively, flinging her arms with wild delight around that grim and withered gaunt black woman. It seemed to me she had never since our marriage embraced me with half the fervour she bestowed upon this hideous old African witch creature.

'Hé, Césarine, it is thee, then, my little one,' the old negress cried out suddenly, in her thin high voice and her muffled Haitian *patois*. 'I did not expect thee so soon, my cabbage. Thou hast come early. Be the welcome one, my granddaughter.'

I reeled with horror as I saw the wrinkled and haggard African kissing once more my beautiful Césarine. It seemed to me a horrible desecration. I had always known, of course, since Césarine was a quadroon, that her grandmother on one side must necessarily have been a full-blooded negress, but I had never yet suspected the reality could be so hideous, so terrible as this.

I crouched down speechless against the paling in my disgust and astonishment, and motioned with my hand to the negro in the hut to remain perfectly quiet. The door of the house closed, and Césarine disappeared: but I waited there, as if chained to the spot, under a hot and burning tropical sun, for fully an hour, unconscious of anything in heaven or earth, save the shock and surprise of that unexpected disclosure.

At last the door opened again, and Césarine apparently came out once more into the neighbouring garden. The gaunt negress followed her close, with one arm thrown caressingly about her beautiful neck and shoulders. In London, Césarine would not have permitted anybody but a great lady to take such a liberty with her; but here in Haiti, she submitted to the old negress's horrid embraces with perfect calmness. Why should she not, indeed! It was her own grandmother.

They came close up to the spot where I was crouching in the thick drifted dust behind the low fence, and then I heard rather than saw that Césarine had flung herself passionately down upon her knees on the ground, and was pouring forth a muttered prayer, in a tongue unknown to me, and full of harsh and uncouth gutturals. It was not Latin; it was not even the coarse Creole French, the negro *patois* in which I heard the people jabbering to one another loudly in the streets around me: it was some still more hideous and barbaric language, a mass of clicks and inarticulate noises, such as I could never have believed might possibly proceed from Césarine's thin and scornful lips.

At last she finished, and I heard her speaking again to her grandmother in the Creole dialect. 'Grandmother, you will pray and get me one. You will not forget me. A boy. A pretty one; an heir to my husband!' It was said wistfully, with an infinite longing. I knew then why she had grown so pale and thin and haggard before we sailed away from England.

The old hag answered in the same tongue, but in her shrill withered note, 'You will bring him up to the religion, my little one, will you?'

Césarine seemed to bow her head. 'I will,' she said. 'He shall follow the religion. Mr. Tristram shall never know anything about it.'

They went back once more into the house, and I crept

away, afraid of being discovered, and returned to the yacht, sick at heart, not knowing how I should ever venture again to meet Césarine.

But when I got back, and had helped myself to a glass of sherry to steady my nerves, from the little flask on Césarine's dressing-table, I thought to myself, hideous as it all seemed, it was very natural Césarine should wish to see her grandmother. After all, was it not better, that proud and haughty as she was, she should not disown her own flesh and blood? And yet, the memory of my beautiful Césarine wrapped in that hideous old black woman's arms made the blood curdle in my very veins.

As soon as Césarine returned, however, gayer and brighter than I had ever seen her, the old fascination overcame me once more, and I determined in my heart to stifle the horror I could not possibly help feeling. And that evening, as I sat alone in the cabin with my wife, I said to her, 'Césarine, we have never spoken about the religious question before: but if it should be ordained we are ever to have any little ones of our own, I should wish them to be brought up in their mother's creed. You could make them better Catholics, I take it, than I could ever make them Christians of any sort.'

Césarine answered never a word, but to my intense surprise she burst suddenly into a flood of tears, and flung herself sobbing on the cabin floor at my feet in an agony of tempestuous cries and writhings.

VII

A few days later, when we had settled down for a three months' stay at a little bungalow on the green hills behind

Port-au-Prince, Césarine said to me early in the day, 'I want to go away to-day, Harry, up into the mountains, to the chapel of Notre Dame de Bon Secours.'

I bowed my head in acquiescence. 'I can guess why you want to go, Reeney,' I answered gently. 'You want to pray there about something that's troubling you. And if I'm not mistaken, it's the same thing that made you cry the other evening when I spoke to you down yonder in the cabin.'

The tears rose hastily once more into Césarine's eyes, and she cried in a low distressed voice, 'Harry, Harry, don't talk to me so. You are too good to me. You will kill me. You will kill me.'

I lifted her head from the table, where she had buried it in her arms, and kissed her tenderly. 'Reeney,' I said, 'I know how you feel, and I hope Notre Dame will listen to your prayers, and send you what you ask of her. But if not, you need never be afraid that I shall love you any the less than I do at present.'

Césarine burst into a fresh flood of tears. 'No, Harry,' she said, 'you don't know about it. You can't imagine it. To us, you know, who have the blood of Africa running in our veins, it is not a mere matter of fancy. It is an eternal disgrace for any woman of our race and descent not to be a mother. I cannot help it. It is the instinct of my people. We are all born so: we cannot feel otherwise.'

It was the only time either of us ever alluded in speaking with one another to the sinister half of Césarine's pedigree.

'You will let me go with you to the mountains, Reeney?' I asked, ignoring her remark. 'You mustn't go so far by yourself, darling.'

'No, Harry, you can't come with me. It would make my prayers ineffectual, dearest. You are a heretic, you know, Harry. You are not Catholic. Notre Dame won't listen to my prayer if I take you with me on my pilgrimage, my darling.'

I saw her mind was set upon it, and I didn't interfere. She would be away all night, she said. There was a rest-house for pilgrims attached to the chapel, and she would be back again at Maisonette (our bungalow) the morning after.

That afternoon she started on her way on a mountain pony I had just bought for her, accompanied only by a negro maid. I couldn't let her go quite unattended through those lawless paths, beset by cottages of half savage Africans; so I followed at a distance, aided by a black groom, and tracked her road along the endless hill-sides up to a fork in the way where the narrow bridle-path divided into two, one of which bore away to leftward, leading, my guide told me, to the chapel of Notre Dame de Bon Secours.

At that point the guide halted. He peered with hand across his eyebrows among the tangled brake of tree-ferns with a terrified look; then he shook his woolly black head ominously. 'I can't go on, Monsieur,' he said, turning to me with an unfeigned shudder. 'Madame has not taken the path of Our Lady. She has gone to the left along the other road, which leads at last to the Vaudoux temple.'

I looked at him incredulously. I had heard before of Vaudoux. It is the hideous African cannibalistic witchcraft of the relapsing half-heathen Haitian Negroes. But Césarine a Vaudoux worshipper! It was too ridiculous. The man must be mistaken; or else Césarine had taken the wrong road by some slight accident.

Next moment, a horrible unspeakable doubt seized upon me irresistibly. What was the unknown shrine in her grandmother's garden at which Césarine had prayed in those awful gutturals? Whatever it was, I would probe this mystery to the very bottom. I would know the truth, come what might of it.

'Go, you coward!' I said to the negro. 'I have no further

need of you. I will make my way alone to the Vaudoux temple.'

'Monsieur,' the man cried, trembling visibly in every limb, 'they will tear you to pieces. If they ever discover you near the temple, they will offer you up as a victim to the Vaudoux.'

'Pooh,' I answered, contemptuous of the fellow's slavish terror. 'Where Madame, a woman dares to go, I, her husband, am certainly not afraid to follow her.'

'Monsieur,' he replied, throwing himself submissively in the dust on the path before me, 'Madame is Creole; she has the blood of the Vaudoux worshippers flowing in her veins. Nobody will hurt her. She is free of the craft. But Monsieur is a pure white and uninitiated. ... If the Vaudoux people catch him at their rites, they will rend him in pieces, and offer his blood as an expiation to the Unspeakable One.'

'Go,' I said, with a smile, turning my horse's head up the right-hand path toward the Vaudoux temple. 'I am not afraid. I will come back again to Maisonette tomorrow.'

I followed the path through a tortuous maze, beset with prickly cactus, agave, and fern-brake, till I came at last to a spur of the hill, where a white wooden building gleamed in front of me, in the full slanting rays of tropical sunset. A skull was fastened to the lintel of the door. I knew at once it was the Vaudoux temple.

I dismounted at once, and led my horse aside into the brake, though I tore his legs and my own as I went with the spines of the cactus plants; and tying him by the bridle to a mountain cabbage palm, in a spot where the thick underbrush completely hid us from view, I lay down and waited patiently for the shades of evening.

It was a moonless night, according to the Vaudoux fashion; and I knew from what I had already read in West

Indian books that the orgies would not commence till midnight.

From time to time, I rubbed a fusee against my hand without lighting it, and by the faint glimmer of the phosphorus on my palm, I was able to read the figures of my watch dial without exciting the attention of the neighbouring Vaudoux worshippers.

Hour after hour went slowly by, and I crouched there still unseen among the agave thicket. At last, as the hands of the watch reached together the point of twelve, I heard a low but deep rumbling noise coming ominously from the Vaudoux temple. I recognized at once the familiar sound. It was the note of the bull-roarer, that mystic instrument of pointed wood, whirled by a string round the head of the hierophant, by whose aid savages in their secret rites summon to their shrines their gods and spirits. I had often made one myself for a toy when I was a boy in England.

I crept out through the tangled brake, and cautiously approached the back of the building. A sentinel was standing by the door in front, a powerful negro, armed with revolver and cutlass. I skulked round noiselessly to the rear, and lifting myself by my hands to the level of the one tiny window, I peered in through a slight scratch on the white paint, with which the glass was covered internally.

I only saw the sight within for a second. Then my brain reeled, and my fingers refused any longer to hold me. But in that second, I had read the whole terrible, incredible truth: I knew what sort of a woman she really was whom I had blindly taken as the wife of my bosom.

Before a rude stone altar covered with stuffed alligator skins, human bones, live snakes, and hideous arts of African superstition, a tall and withered black woman stood erect, naked as she came from her mother's womb, one skinny arm raised aloft, and the other holding below some dark object, that writhed and struggled awfully in her hand on the slab of the altar, even as she held it. I saw in a flash of the torches behind it was the black hag I had watched before at the Port-au-Prince cottage.

Beside her, whiter of skin, and faultless of figure, stood a younger woman, beautiful to behold, imperious and haughty still, like a Greek statue, unmoved before that surging horrid background of naked black and cringing savages. Her head was bent, and her hand pressed convulsively against the swollen veins in her throbbing brow; and I saw at once it was my own wife – a Vaudoux worshipper – Césarine Tristram.

In another flash, I knew the black woman had a sharp flint knife in her uplifted hand; and the dark object in the other hand I recognized with a thrill of unspeakable horror as a Negro girl of four years old or thereabouts, gagged and bound, and lying on the altar.

Before I could see the sharp flint descend upon the naked breast of the writhing victim, my fingers in mercy refused to bear me, and I fell half fainting on the ground below, too shocked and unmanned even to crawl away at once out of reach of the awful unrealizable horror.

But by the sounds within, I knew they had completed their hideous sacrifice, and that they were smearing over Césarine – my own wife – the woman of my choice – with the warm blood of the human victim.

Sick and faint, I crept away slowly through the tangled underbrush, tearing my skin as I went with the piercing cactus spines; untied my horse from the spot where I had fastened him; and rode him down without drawing rein, cantering round sharp angles and down horrible ledges, till he stood at last, white with foam, by the grey dawn, in front of the little piazza at Maisonette.

VIII

That night, the thunder roared and the lightning played with tropical fierceness round the tall hilltops away in the direction of the Vaudoux temple. The rain came down in fearful sheets, and the torrents roared and foamed in cataracts, and tore away great gaps in the rough paths on the steep hillsides. But at eight o'clock in the morning Césarine returned, drenched with wet, and with a strange frown upon her haughty forehead.

I did not know how to look at her or how to meet her.

'My prayers are useless,' she muttered angrily as she entered. 'Some heretic must have followed me unseen to the chapel of Notre Dame de Bon Secours. The pilgrimage is a failure.'

'You are wet,' I said, trembling. 'Change your things, Césarine.' I could not pretend to speak gently to her.

She turned upon me with a fierce look in her big black eyes. Her instinct showed her at once I had discovered her secret. 'Tell them, and hang me,' she cried fiercely.

It was what the law required me to do. I was otherwise the accomplice of murder and cannibalism. But I could not do it. Profoundly as I loathed her and hated her presence, now, I couldn't find it in my heart to give her up to justice, as I knew I ought to do.

I turned away and answered nothing.

Presently, she came out again from her bedroom, with her wet things still dripping around her. 'Smoke that,' she said, handing me a tiny cigarette rolled round in a leaf of fresh tobacco.

'I will not,' I answered with a vague surmise, taking it from her fingers. 'I know the smell. It is manchineal. You cannot any longer deceive me.'

She went back to her bedroom once more. I sat, dazed and stupefied, in the bamboo chair on the front piazza. What to do, I knew not, and cared not. I was tied to her for life, and there was no help for it, save by denouncing her to the rude Haitian justice.

In an hour or more, our English maid came out to speak to me. 'I'm afraid sir,' she said, 'Mrs. Tristram is getting delirious. She seems to be in a high fever. Shall I ask one of these poor black bodies to go out and get the English doctor?'

I went into my wife's bedroom. Césarine lay moaning piteously on the bed, in her wet clothes still; her cheeks were hot, and her pulse was high and thin and feverish. I knew without asking what was the matter with her. It was yellow fever.

The night's exposure in that terrible climate, and the ghastly scene she had gone through so intrepidly, had broken down even Césarine's iron constitution.

I sent for the doctor and had her put to bed immediately. The black nurse and I undressed her between us. We found next her bosom, tied by a small red silken thread, a tiny bone, fresh and ruddy-looking. I knew what it was, and so did the Negress. It was a human finger-bone – the last joint of a small child's fourth finger. The Negress shuddered and hid her head. 'It is Vaudoux, Monsieur!' she said. 'I have seen it on others. Madame has been paying a visit, I suppose, to her grandmother.'

For six long endless days and nights I watched and nursed that doomed criminal, doing everything for her that skill could direct or care could suggest to me: yet all the time fearing and dreading that she might yet recover, and not knowing in my heart what either of our lives could ever be like if she did live through it.

A merciful Providence willed it otherwise.

On the sixth day, the fatal *vomito Negro* set in – the symptom of the last incurable stage of yellow fever – and I knew for certain that Césarine would die. She had brought her own punishment upon her. At midnight that evening she died delirious.

Thank God, she had left no child of mine behind her to inherit the curse her mother's blood had handed down to her!

IX

On my return to London, whither I went by mail direct, leaving the yacht to follow after me, I drove straight to the Lathams' from Waterloo Station. Mrs. Latham was out, the servant said, But Miss Irene was in the drawing-room.

Irene was sitting at the window by herself, working quietly at a piece of crewel work. She rose to meet me with her sweet simple little English smile. I took her hand and pressed it like a brother.

'I got your telegram,' she said simply. 'Harry, I know she is dead; but I know something terrible besides has happened. Tell me all. Don't be afraid to speak of it before me. I am not afraid, for my part, to listen.'

I sat down on the sofa beside her, and told her all, without one word of excuse or concealment, from our last parting to the day of Césarine's death in Haiti: and she held my hand and listened all the while with breathless wonderment to my strange story.

At the end I said, 'Irene, it has all come and gone between us like a hideous nightmare. I cannot imagine even now how that terrible woman, with all her power, could ever for one moment have bewitched me away from you, my beloved, my queen, my own heart's darling.'

Irene did not try to hush me or to stop me in any way. She merely sat and looked at me steadily, and said nothing.

'It was fascination,' I cried. 'Infatuation, madness, delirium, enchantment.'

'It was worse than that, Harry,' Irene answered, rising quietly. 'It was poison; it was witchcraft; it was sheer African devilry.'

In a flash of thought, I remembered the cup of coffee at Seymour Crescent, the curious sherry at Port-au-Prince, the cigarette with the manchineal she had given me on the mountains, and I saw forthwith that Irene with her woman's quickness had divined rightly. It was more than infatuation; it was intoxication with African charms and West Indian poisons.

'What a man does in such a woman's hands is not his own doing,' Irene said slowly. 'He has no more control of himself in such circumstances than if she had drugged him with chloroform or opium.'

'Then you forgive me, Irene?'

'I have nothing to forgive, Harry. I am grieved for you. I am frightened.' Then bursting into tears, 'My darling, my darling; I love you, I love you!'

THE DEMON SPELL

by Hume Nisbet

Towards the end of 1888, London, and particularly the East End, was plunged into a very real Reign of Terror by a series of gruesome murders in the Whitechapel district. The name given to the elusive perpetrator of these savage crimes has become immortal: Jack the Ripper.*

Estimates of the exact number of murders committed by the Ripper vary but it was probably not more than six. So common were crimes of violence among the East End's 'People of the Abyss', as Jack London called them, that many murders went unpublicized and it is not clear why these particular murders should so have inflamed the popular imagination and become eventual legend. The probable reason is that most of the victims were prostitutes, belonging to a profession whose very existence was denied by many of the Victorian middle-class – at least publicly. The murders, made more shocking by the sexual nature of the mutilations, brought home the sordid social conditions prevailing at the heart of the Empire with an impact that could not be ignored. As one murder succeeded another, panic became widespread and the Queen herself was moved to invite

---

* The name originates in a letter, purporting to be from the murderer, which the Central News Agency received: 'I am down on whores and shant quit ripping them till I do get buckled.'

officers in charge of the case to the Palace to hear her own suggestions for the apprehension of the fiend responsible. One fortunate consequence of the atrocities was that outraged public concern forced improvements in the conditions of London's poor.

Theories as to the identity of the Ripper were legion, and continue to be, and it was not long before such conjectures entered the domain of fiction.* The appalling nature of the injuries inflicted on the victims led some to suppose that the murderer could hardly be human. In The Demon Spell, *written only a few years after the murders, Hume Nisbet takes this hypothesis to its ultimate conclusion.*

A Scottish painter and illustrator, Nisbet spent many years travelling through unsettled parts of Australia and New Guinea.

These experiences he put to use in novels like A Bush Girl's Romance *and* The Bushranger's Sweetheart. *Most of his novels were adventure stories:* Valdmer the Viking; Children of the Hermes; Comrades of the Black Cross; The Jolly Roger *and* The Great Secret, 'a novel of tomorrow'. *Yet he also produced two collections of excellent tales of horror –* Stories Weird and Wonderful *and* The Haunted Station. *It is from the latter that I have chosen this dark tale of lurking evil.*

IT was about the time when spiritualism was all the craze in England, and no party was reckoned complete without a spirit-rapping séance being included amongst the other entertainments.

One night I had been invited to the house of a friend, who was a great believer in the manifestations from the unseen

* More stories on the theme of the Ripper murders are contained in my anthology *Jack the Knife* (Mayflower Books, 1975).

88

world, and who had asked for my special edification a well-known trance medium. 'A pretty as well as a heaven-gifted girl, whom you will be sure to like, I know,' he said as he asked me.

I did not believe much in the return of spirits, yet, thinking to be amused, consented to attend at the hour appointed. At that time I had just returned from a long sojourn abroad, and was in a very delicate state of health, easily impressed by outward influences, and nervous to a most extraordinary extent.

To the hour appointed I found myself at my friend's house, and was then introduced to the sitters who had assembled to witness the phenomena. Some were strangers like myself to the rules of the table, others who were adepts took their places at once in the order to which they had in former meetings attended. The trance medium had not yet arrived, and while waiting upon her coming we sat down and opened the séance with a hymn.

We had just furnished the second verse when the door opened and the medium glided in, and took her place on a vacant seat by my side, joining with the others in the last verse, after which we all sat motionless with our hands resting upon the table, waiting upon the first manifestation from the unseen world.

Now, although I thought all this performance very ridiculous, there was something in the silence and the dim light, for the gas had been turned low down, and the room seemed filled with shadows; something about the fragile figure at my side, with her drooping head, which thrilled me with a curious sense of fear and icy horror such as I had never felt before.

I am not by nature imaginative or inclined to superstition, but, from the moment that young girl had entered the room, I felt as if a hand had been laid upon my heart, a cold iron hand, that was compressing it, and causing it to stop throbbing. My sense of hearing also had grown more acute and sensitive, so that the beating of the watch in my vest pocket sounded like the thumping of a quartz-crushing machine, and the measured breathing of those about me as loud and nerve-disturbing as the snorting of a steam engine.

Only when I turned to look upon the trance medium did I become soothed; then it seemed as if a cold-air wave had passed through my brain, subduing, for the time being, those awful sounds.

'She is possessed,' whispered my host on the other side of me. 'Wait, and she will speak presently, and tell us whom we have got beside us.'

As we sat and waited the table had moved several times under our hands, while knockings at intervals took place in the table and all round the room, a most weird and blood-curdling, yet ridiculous performance, which made me feel half inclined to run out with fear, and half inclined to sit still and laugh; on the whole, I think, however, that horror had the more complete possession of me.

Presently she raised her head and laid her hand upon mine, beginning to speak in a strange monotonous, far away voice, 'This is my first visit since I passed from earth-life, and *you* have called me here.'

I shivered as her hand touched mine, but had no strength to withdraw it from her light, soft grasp.

'I am what you would call a lost soul; that is, I am in the lowest sphere. Last week I was in the body, but met my death down Whitechapel way. I was what you call an unfortunate, aye, unfortunate enough. Shall I tell you how it happened?'

The medium's eyes were closed, and whether it was my distorted imagination or not, she appeared to have grown older and decidedly debauched-looking since she sat down, or rather as if a light, filmy mask of degrading and soddened vice had replaced the former delicate features.

No one spoke, and the trance medium continued:

'I had been out all that day and without any luck or food, so that I was dragging my wearied body along through the slush and mud, for it had been wet all day, and I was drenched to the skin, and miserable, ah, ten thousand times more wretched than I am now, for the earth is a far worse hell for such as I than our hell here.

'I had importuned several passers by as I went along that night, but none of them spoke to me, for work had been scarce all this winter, and I suppose I did not look so tempting as I have been; only once a man answered me, a dark-faced, middle-sized man, with a soft voice, and much better dressed than my usual companions.

'He asked me where I was going, and then left me, putting a coin into my hand, for which I thanked him. Being just in time for the last public-house, I hurried up, but on going to the bar and looking at my hand, I found it to be a curious foreign coin, with outlandish figures on it, which the landlord would not take, so I went out again to the dark fog and rain without my drink after all.

'There was no use going any further that night. I turned up the court where my lodgings were, intending to go home and get a sleep, since I could get no food, when I felt something touch me softly from behind like as if someone had caught hold of my shawl; then I stopped and turned about to see who it was.

'I was alone, and with no one near me, nothing but fog and the half light from the court lamp. Yet I felt as if something had got hold of me, though I could not see what it was, and that it was gathering about me.

'I tried to scream out, but could not, as this unseen grasp

closed upon my throat and choked me, and then I fell down and for a moment forgot everything.

'Next moment I woke up, outside my own poor mutilated body, and stood watching the fell work going on – as you see it now.'

Yes I saw it all as the medium ceased speaking, a mangled corpse lying on a muddy pavement, and a demoniac, dark, pock-marked face bending over it, with the lean claws outspread, and the dense fog instead of a body, like the half-formed incarnation of muscles.

'That is what did it, and you will know it again,' she said, 'I have come for you to find it.'

'Is he an Englishman?' I gasped, as the vision faded away and the room once more became definite.

'It is neither man nor woman, but it lives as I do, it is with me now and may be with you to-night, still if you will have me instead of it, I can keep it back, only you must wish for *me* with all your might.'

The séance was now becoming too horrible, and by general consent our host turned up the gas, and then I saw for the first time the medium, now relieved from her evil possession, a beautiful girl of about nineteen, with I think the most glorious brown eyes I had ever before looked into.

'Do you believe what you have been speaking about?' I asked her as we were sitting talking together.

'What was that?'

'About the murdered woman.'

'I don't know anything at all, only that I have been sitting at the table. I never know what my trances are.'

Was she speaking the truth? Her dark eyes looked truth, so that I could not doubt her.

That night when I went to my lodgings I must confess that it was some time before I could make up my mind to go to bed. I was decidedly upset and nervous, and wished that I had never gone to this spirit meeting, making a mental vow, as I threw off my clothes and hastily got into bed, that it was the last unholy gathering I would ever attend.

For the first time in my life I could not put out the gas, I felt as if the room was filled with ghosts, as if this pair of ghastly spectres, the murderer and his victim, had accompanied me home, and were at that moment disputing the possession of me, so instead, I pulled the bedclothes over my head, it being a cold night, and went that fashion off to sleep.

Twelve o'clock! and the anniversary of the day that Christ was born. Yes, I heard it striking from the street spire and counted the strokes, slowly tolled out, listening to the echoes from other steeples, after this one had ceased, as I lay awake in that gas-lit room, feeling as if I was not alone this Christmas morn.

Thus, while I was trying to think what had made me wake so suddenly, I seemed to hear a far off echo cry 'Come to me.' At the same time the bedclothes were slowly pulled from the bed, and left in a confused mass on the floor.

'Is that you, Polly?' I cried, remembering the spirit séance, and the name by which the spirit had announced herself when she took possession.

Three distinct knocks resounded on the bedpost at my ear, the signal for 'Yes.'

'Can you speak to me?'

'Yes,' an echo rather than a voice replied, while I felt my flesh creeping, yet strove to be brave.

'Can I see you?'

'No!'

'Feel you?'

Instantly the feeling of a light cold hand touched my brow and passed over my face.

'In God's name what do you want?'

'To save the girl I was *in* tonight. *It* is after her and will kill her if you do not come quickly.'

In an instant I was out of the bed, and tumbling my clothes on any way, horrified through it all, yet feeling as if Polly were helping me to dress. There was a Kandian dagger on my table which I had brought from Ceylon, an old dagger which I had bought for its antiquity and design, and this I snatched up as I left the room, with that light unseen hand leading me out of the house and along the deserted snow-covered streets.

I did not know where the trance medium lived, but I followed where that light grasp led me, through the wild, blinding snow-drift, round corners and through short cuts, with my head down and the flakes falling thickly about me, until at last I arrived at a silent square and in front of a house, which by some instinct, I knew that I must enter.

Over by the other side of the street I saw a man standing looking up to a dimly-lighted window, but I could not see him very distinctly and I did not pay much attention to him at the time, but rushed instead up the front steps and into the house, that unseen hand still pulling me forward.

How that door opened, or if it did open I could not say, I only know that I got in, as we get into places in a dream, and up the inner stairs, I passed into a bedroom where the light was burning dimly.

It was her bedroom, and she was struggling in the thug-like grasp of those same demon claws, and the rest of it drifting away to nothingness.

I saw it all at a glance, her half-naked form, with the disarranged bedclothes, as the unformed demon of muscles clutched that delicate throat, and then I was at it like a fury with my Kandian dagger, slashing crossways at those cruel claws and that evil face, while blood streaks followed the course of my knife, making ugly stains, until at last it ceased struggling and disappeared like a horrid nightmare, as the half-strangled girl, now released from that fell grip, woke up the house with her screams, while from her relaxing hand dropped a strange coin, which I took possession of.

Thus I left her, feeling that my work was done, going downstairs as I had come up, without impediment or even seemingly, in the slightest degree, attracting the attention of the other inmates of the house, who rushed in their night-dresses towards the bedroom from whence the screams were issuing.

Into the street again, with that coin in one hand and my dagger in the other I rushed, and then I remembered the man whom I had seen looking up at the window. Was he there still? Yes, but on the ground in a confused black mass amongst the white snow as if he had been struck down.

I went over to where he lay and looked at him. Was he dead? Yes. I turned him round and saw that his throat was gashed from ear to ear, and all over his face – the same dark, pallid, pock-marked evil face, and claw-like hands, I saw the dark slashes of my Kandian dagger, while the soft white snow around him was stained with crimson life pools, and as I looked I heard the clock strike one, while from the distance sounded the chant of the coming waits, then I turned and fled blindly into the darkness.

A MYSTERIOUS VISITOR

by Mrs. Henry Wood

In these days of instant communications it is sometimes difficult to conceive of the terrors to which the Victorians were prone. Take, for instance, the plight of the common soldier shipped off to defend the Empire in places like Zululand and Afghanistan which must have seemed as remote as the planets; places where the climate was intolerable, disease rife and the local natives treated prisoners with a cruelty that was hardly credible. India, at least, seemed half-civilized so the consternation at home was that much greater when, in 1857, Indian troops mutinied against their officers and slaughtered large numbers of British including women and children. This is the background of A Mysterious Visitor *which demonstrates that, whatever attitudes exist to-day regarding Victorian Imperialism, the Empire was neither easily won nor easily retained.*

Mrs. Henry Wood (1814–1887) started life as Ellen Price. After her marriage in 1836 she wrote only under the name by which she is best known. Her early contributions to Bentley's Miscellany *and the* New Monthly Magazine *proved very popular and her work became much in demand by the magazines.* Danesbury House, *her first novel, sold only moderately well but* East Lynne *published the following year was an overwhelming success and met with still greater success as a stage-play. Although now wealthy Mrs Wood persevered with her literary interests and from 1867 was editor/owner of* The Argosy.

Mrs. Wood was an opponent of the Socialist movement and wrote an anonymous anti-Labour novel, A Life's Secret, *the publication of which precipitated riots and threats against the author's life. Probably her chief talent lay in her ability to realistically depict middle class characters – a talent fully displayed in* A Mysterious Visitor.

ON Monday morning, the 11th of May, 1857 – the year, as the reader may remember, that England was destined to be shaken to its centre with the disastrous news of the rising in India – there sat in one of the quiet rooms of Enton Parsonage a young and pretty woman, playing with her baby. It was Mrs. Ordie. The incumbent of Enton was Dr. Ling, an honorary canon of the county cathedral. Mrs. Ling was from India: her family connections, uncles, brothers, and cousins, had been, or were, in the civil or military service of Bengal. Consequently, as the daughters of Dr. Ling had grown towards womanhood, they were severally shipped off, with high matrimonial views, according to a fashion that extensively prevails.

Miss Ling, Louisa, had gone out first, and had secured Captain Ordie. Constance went next, and espoused Lieutenant Main, to the indignation of all her relatives, both at home and out, for she was a handsome girl, and had been set down for nothing less than a major. The third daughter, Sarah Ann, very young and pretty she was, went out the following year, with a stern injunction not to do as Constance had done.

Before Sarah Ann could get there, Mrs. Ordie's health failed, and she was ordered immediately to her native climate. Upon landing, she proceeded to Enton. The voyage had been of much service to her, and her health was improved. And there we see her sitting, on the morning of the 11th of May, nearly twelve months after her arrival, playing with her infant, who was nine months old. In August she and the child were going back to India.

Mrs. Ordie was much attached to this child, very anxious and fidgety over it: her first child had died in India. She fancied, this morning, that it was not well, and had been sending in haste for Mrs. Beecher, who lived close by, just beyond the garden. The honorary canon and the rest of the family had gone to spend a week in the county town.

Mrs. Beecher came in without her bonnet. She had been governess to Louisa and Constance, had married the curate, and remained the deeply-attached friend and adviser of the Ling family. In any emergency Mrs. Beecher was appealed to.

'I am sure baby's ill,' was Mrs. Ordie's salutation. 'I have been doing all I can to excite her notice, but she will keep her head down. See how hot her cheeks are.'

'I think she is sleepy,' said Mrs. Beecher. 'And perhaps a very little feverish.'

'*Do* you think her feverish? What shall I do? Good mercy, if she should die as my other baby did!'

'Louisa,' remonstrated Mrs. Beecher, 'do not excite yourself causelessly. I thought you had left that habit off.'

'Oh, but you don't know what it is to lose a child; you never had one,' returned Mrs. Ordie, giving way to her excitement. 'If she does, I can tell you I shall die with her.'

'Hush,' interrupted Mrs. Beecher. 'I believe there is little, if anything, the matter with the child, excepting her teeth, which renders children somewhat feverish. But if she were dangerously ill, you have no right to say what you have just said.'

'Oh yes, I have a right, for it is truth. I would rather lose everything I possess in the world, than my baby. What a long while Mr. Percival is!' she added, walking to the window and looking out.

'You surely have not sent for Mr. Percival?'

'I surely have. And if he does not soon make his appearance, I shall send again.'

Mrs. Ordie had always been of most excitable temperament. As a girl, her imagination was so vivid, so prone to the marvellous, that story books and fairy tales were kept from her. She would get them unknown to her parents, and wake up in the night, shrieking with terror at what she had read. Hers was indeed a peculiarly active brain. It is necessary to mention this, as it may account, in some degree, for what follows.

There was really nothing the matter with the child, but Mrs. Ordie insisted that there was, and made herself miserable all the day. The surgeon, Mr. Percival, came: he saw little the matter with it either, but he ordered it a warm bath, and sent in some medicine – probably distilled water and sugar. Mrs. Beecher came in again in the evening. Mrs. Ordie hinted that she might as well remain for the night, to be on the spot should baby be taken worse.

The curate's wife laughed. 'I think I can promise you that there will be no danger, Louisa. You may cease to torment yourself, and go to sleep in peace.'

'If anything does happen, I shall send to call you up.'

The Lings kept four servants. Two of these, a man and maid, were with their master and mistress; the other two were at home. And there was also the child's nurse. After Mrs. Beecher left, Mrs. Ordie crept along the corridor to the nurse's room, where the baby slept, and found the nurse undressing herself.

'What are you doing that for?' she indignantly exclaimed.

'Of course you will sit up to-night, and watch my baby.'

'Sit up for what, ma'am?' returned the nurse.

'I would not leave the child unwatched to-night for anything. My other baby died of convulsions; they may also attack this one. Convulsions are so uncertain: they come on in a moment. I have ordered Martha to sit up in the kitchen and keep hot water in readiness.'

'Why, ma'am, there's no cause in the world for it,' remonstrated the surprised nurse. 'The baby is as well as well can be, and has never woke up since I laid her down at eight o'clock.'

'She shall be watched this night,' persisted Mrs. Ordie. 'So dress yourself again.'

'I must say it's a shame,' grumbled the nurse, who had grown tired of her mistress's capricious ways, and had privately told the other servants that she did not care how soon she left the situation. 'I'd remain up for a week, if there was need of it, but to be deprived of one's natural rest for nothing, ma'am, is too bad. I'll sit myself in the old rocking-chair, if I must stay up,' added the servant, half to herself, half to her mistress, 'and get a sleep that way.'

Mrs. Ordie's eyes flashed anger. The fact was, the slavery of Eastern servants had a little spoiled her for the independence of European ones. She accused the girl of every crime that was unfeeling, short of child murder, and concluded by having the infant's crib carried down to her own room. She would sit up herself and watch it.

The child still slept calmly and quietly, and Mrs. Ordie sat quietly by it. But she began to find it rather dull, and she went to the book-shelves and took down a book. It was then striking eleven. Setting the lamp on a small table at her elbow, she began to read.

She had taken the 'Vicar of Wakefield'. She had not opened the book for years, and she read on with interest, all her old pleasure in the tale revived. Nearly half-an-hour had elapsed when she suddenly heard footsteps on the gravel-path outside, advancing towards the house, and she looked up and listened. The first thought that struck her was, that one of the servants had been out without permission, and was coming in at that late hour; which, as her watch, hanging opposite, told her, was twenty-five minutes past eleven. But she had not heard the bell ring. It must be explained that Enton Parsonage stood back from the high-road and was surrounded by trees. Two iron gates gave ingress to it from the road. They were far apart, for the house was low and long; the kitchens, forming a right angle with the house, projected out, their windows looking sideways on the broad half-circular gravel-path that led from one gate to the other. The entrance-porch was near the kitchens. At the back of the house stood the smaller house of the curate; a narrow pathway leading to it from the Parsonage. *That* house faced the side lane, into which lane its small iron gate opened. These gates, the Rector's two large ones and the curate's small one, were always locked at sunset, and the premises were then deemed secure. There was no other entrance to them whatever, and all three gates were lofty and spiked at the top, preventing the possibility of any marauder's climbing over. If any friends came to either of the two houses after the gates were locked, they had to ring for admittance.

Mrs. Ordie heard these footsteps in the stillness of the night, and her eyes instantly glanced at her watch. Twenty-five minutes after eleven. Who was it, at this late hour? But, even as the question passed through her mind, an expression of astonishment rose to her face; her eyes dilated, she drew in her breath and listened intently. If ever she heard the footsteps of her husband, she thought she heard them then.

Yes, yes! It was impossible to mistake his sharp, firm

step, which she had never heard since she left him in Calcutta. It was very close now, nearly underneath her window. With a cry of joy she arose and opened it.

'George, dear George! I knew your step. What has brought you home?'

There was no answer. The footsteps were still advancing, and Mrs. Ordie leaned out. He had come in at the further gate, had passed along the front of the house, and was now underneath her window. She saw him distinctly in the light cast on the path from the kitchen. There was no mistaking him for any other than Captain Ordie, and he wore his regimentals. He lifted his face, she saw it clearly in the light, and looked at her. Then he went on and stepped inside the porch. She called to him again.

'George, you did not hear me. Don't knock, baby's ill. Wait a moment, and I will let you in.'

Closing the window, she sprang to the door. Her lamp was not suitable for carrying, and she would not stay to light a taper: she knew every stair well. But she was awkward at the fastenings of the front-door, and found she could not undo them in the dark, so ran into the kitchen. The cook, sitting up in obedience to her orders, was lying back in a chair, her feet stretched out upon another. She was fast asleep and snoring. A large fire burnt in the grate, and two candles were alight on the ironing-board underneath the window.

'Martha! Martha!' she exclaimed, 'rouse yourself. My husband's come.'

'What!' cried the woman, starting up in affright, and evidently forgetting where she was. 'Who's come, ma'am?'

'Come and open the hall-door. Captain Ordie is there.'

She snatched one of the candles from the table, and went on to the door again. The servant followed, rubbing her eyes.

The door was unlocked and thrown open, and Mrs. Ordie

drew a little back to give space for him to enter. No one came in. Mrs. Ordie looked out then, holding the candle above her head. She could not see him anywhere.

'Take the light,' she said to the maid, and stepped beyond the portico. 'George!' she called out, 'where are you? The door is open.' But Captain Ordie neither appeared nor answered.

'Well, I never knew such an extraordinary thing!'

'Ma'am,' said the servant, who began now to be pretty well awake, 'I don't understand. Did you say anybody was come?'

'My husband is come. Captain Ordie.'

'From Mrs. Beecher's?' asked the woman.

'Mrs. Beecher's, no! What should bring him at Mrs. Beecher's? He must have come direct from Portsmouth.'

'But he must have come to the door here from the Beechers',' continued the servant. 'He couldn't have come any other way. The gates are locked, ma'am!'

In her wonder at his appearance, this fact had not struck Mrs. Ordie. 'One of them must have been left unfastened,' she said, after thinking. 'That was very careless, Martha. It is your place to see to it, when Richard is out. Papa once turned a servant away for leaving the gates open at night.'

'I locked both the gates at sundown,' was the woman's reply. 'And the key's hanging up in its place in the kitchen.'

'Impossible,' thought Mrs. Ordie. 'Where is Susan?' – alluding to the other servant at home.

'Susan went to bed at ten o'clock, ma'am.'

'It is not possible that the gates can have been locked, Martha. The captain came in by the upper one, the furthest from here. I heard him the minute he put his foot on the gravel, and knew his step. You must have thought you locked them. George!' added Mrs. Ordie, in a louder tone. 'George!'

There was no answer. No sound whatever broke the stillness of the night.

'Captain Ordie!' she repeated. 'Captain Ordie!'

The servant was laughing to herself, taking care that her young mistress did not see her. She believed that Mrs. Ordie had dropped asleep, and had *dreamt* she heard somebody on the gravel.

'I know what it is,' cried Mrs. Ordie, briskly. 'He has never been here before; and, finding the door was not immediately opened to him, has gone on to Mr. Beecher's, thinking this the wrong house.'

She ran down the narrow path as she spoke, which branched off round by the kitchen-window; the maid followed her. It was a light night.

But nothing was to be seen of George Ordie. The curate's house, a small one, presented the appearance of a dwelling whose inmates are at rest; the blinds were drawn before the windows, and all was still. Mrs. Ordie ran over probabilities in her mind, and came to the conclusion that he could not have gone there. The Beechers were early people, and had no doubt been in bed an hour ago. Had her husband knocked there, he would be waiting at the door still, for they had not had time to come down and let him in.

'It could only have been fancy, ma'am,' cried Martha.

'Silence,' said Mrs. Ordie. 'How can it have been fancy? I heard my husband, and saw him.'

'Well, ma'am, I argue so from the gates being fast. He couldn't have got over 'em, because of the spikes.'

'The gates cannot be fast,' returned Mrs. Ordie, 'and it is foolish of you to persist in saying so – only to screen your own carelessness.'

'I wish you'd just please to look at the gates,' retorted Martha.

'I will,' said Mrs. Ordie, anxious to convict Martha to her

face. 'It is an utter impossibility that Captain Ordie can have come in at a high, locked gate, with spikes on the top; he would not attempt to do so. He would have rung the bell.'

'That's what I say,' answered Martha. 'I dreamt t'other night,' she muttered, as she followed her mistress, 'that a man came down that there path with lovely gownd pieces to sell: I might just as well have riz up the house, and had *him* looked for.'

They gained the broad walk, and proceeded round towards the further gate. It was locked. Martha sniffed.

'Why, it is like magic!' uttered Mrs. Ordie.

'I was certain about its being locked, ma'am. And that's why I say it must be fancy.'

Mrs. Ordie was indignant. 'Is this gate fancy?' she said, shaking it, in her anger. 'Don't tell me again that my husband is fancy. How could I have seen and heard him if he were not come? Captain Ordie!' she called out, once more. 'George! where can you have gone to?'

'Come to the other gate, Martha.'

They retraced their steps, Mrs. Ordie looking in all directions for a gleam of scarlet, and reached the other gate. It was locked. Mr. Beecher's gate was locked. Then she went about the garden, and looked and called: but there was no trace of Captain Ordie. The servant walked with her, half amused, half provoked.

'Can he have slipped indoors,' murmured Mrs. Ordie, 'while we went round to the Beechers?' And she went in to look, taking the opportunity to glance at her child. But Captain Ordie was nowhere to be seen, and she had never been so much perplexed and puzzled in all her life.

'Then he must have gone on, as I thought, to Mr. Beecher's,' was her last solution of the enigma. 'They were possibly up, and let him in directly. And they are keeping him there till morning, that he may not disturb us, knowing that baby is ill.'

'But about the gate,' interrupted the servant, returning to her stumbling-block, 'how could he have got through it?'

'I know he did get through it, and that's enough,' responded Mrs. Ordie, disposing summarily of the difficulty. 'Soldiers are venturesome and can do anything. I will go and fetch him. You stop here, Martha, and listen to baby.'

Once more Mrs. Ordie sped to the curate's. She knocked at the door, and stood back to look up at the house. 'They have put him into their spare bed,' she soliloquized; 'Mrs. Beecher has kept it made up this fortnight past, expecting their invalid from India. My goodness! I never thought of it! they have no doubt come together, in the same ship. George may have gone to Calcutta; and, finding James Beecher was coming, must have got leave, all in a hurry, and accompanied him.'

Picking up some bits of gravel, she threw them at Mrs. Beecher's bedroom-window. This brought forth the curate in his night-cap, peeping through the curtains.

'It is I, Mr. Beecher. Have you got Captain Ordie here?'

'Make haste, Anne,' cried the curate, turning his head round to speak to his wife. 'It is Mrs. Ordie. Perhaps the child is in a fit.'

'My husband,' repeated Mrs. Ordie. 'He is here, is he not?'

'Yes; directly,' answered the curate, imperfectly understanding, but opening the casement about an inch to speak.

'Is she really worse, Louisa?' exclaimed Mrs. Beecher, who now appeared at the window. 'I will soon be with you.'

The curate, believing the matter to be settled, drew in his night-cap. But Mrs. Ordie's voice was again heard. 'Mr. Beecher! I want you.'

'Dress yourself, my dear,' cried Mrs. Beecher to him, in a

flurry. 'I dare say they want you to go for Mr. Percival. If the baby is really worse, and it is not Louisa's fancy, I shall never more boast of knowing children. She is calling again.'

Mr. Beecher reopened the casement. 'I am putting on my clothes, Mrs. Ordie. I am coming.'

'But you need not do that. Has your brother arrived?'

'Who?'

'Your brother: James Beecher.'

'No. Not yet.'

'Some ship is in: it has brought my husband. Tell him I am here.'

'We'll be down in a minute,' called out Mr. Beecher, and making desperate haste. 'Anne, Captain Ordie's come.'

'Captain Ordie!' exclaimed Mrs. Beecher.

'Mrs. Ordie says so.'

'Then we shall have James here to-morrow. How very unexpected Captain Ordie's arrival must have been to his wife? And to find his child ill!'

Louisa Ordie waited. Mrs. Beecher came down first, in a large shawl, her bonnet tied over her night-cap. They began to speak at cross-purposes.

'Is he coming? Have you told him?' impatiently asked Mrs. Ordie.

'My dear, yes. But he had gone upstairs in slippers, and his shoes were in the back-kitchen. Captain Ordie's arrival must have taken you by surprise.'

'I never was so much surprised in my life,' answered Mrs. Ordie, standing still, and not offering to stir. 'I heard his footstep first, and knew it, even in the distance. I am so glad! He must have come with James Beecher.'

'Ay, we shall have James here to-morrow. But, my dear, let us not lose time. Is the child very ill?'

'She is not worse; there is no hurry,' answered Mrs. Ordie, planting her back against a tree, as deliberately as if she meant to make it her station for the night, and gazing up at the casement which she knew belonged to their spare bedroom. Mrs. Beecher looked at her in surprise.

'Will he be long?' she resumed. 'There's no light.'

'He will be here directly,' said Mrs. Beecher; 'he is finding his shoes. I suppose Kitty put them in some out-of-the-way place, ready for cleaning in the morning.'

Another pause, and the curate appeared.

'Oh, Mr. Beecher, *you* need not have got up,' was Mrs. Ordie's greeting. 'I am sorry to give you all this trouble.'

'It is no trouble. Do you want me to go for Mr. Percival?'

'You are very kind, but we shall not require the doctor tonight: at least I hope not. I have been watching her myself: I had her brought down to my own room. Nurse behaved shamefully over it, and I gave her warning.'

'Pray let us go and see how she is,' said Mrs. Beecher, never supposing but they had been called up by the state of the child.

'When he comes. You say he will not be long. Had he undressed?'

'Had who undressed?'

'My husband.'

Mrs. Beecher stared at her in amazement. 'I do not understand you, Louisa. For whom are we waiting here?'

'For my husband, of course. You say he is finding his shoes.'

Both Mr. and Mrs. Beecher thought her child's illness was turning her crazy. They looked at her, and at one another.

'My dear, you are mystifying us,' spoke the wife, drawing her shawl tighter round her shoulders. 'Is your husband coming out here; into the garden? Are we to wait here for him?'

'Why, you know he is coming out, and of course I shall wait for him. Only think, he wore his regimentals!'

'His regimentals!'

'Yes. Just as if he were on duty.'

'Where is Captain Ordie?' interposed the curate.

'Well, that's a sensible question, from you,' laughed Mrs. Ordie. 'I suppose he is in your spare bedroom, though I see no light. Or else hunting for his shoes in your kitchen.'

'Child,' said Mrs. Beecher, taking hold of her tenderly, 'you are not well. I told you to-day what it would be, if you excited yourself. Let us take you home.'

'I will not go without my husband. There. And what makes him so long? I shall call to him. Why, you have locked the door!' she exclaimed. 'You have locked him in.'

'Locked who in, child?' said Mrs. Beecher. 'There's no one in the house but Kitty.'

'My husband is there. Did he not come to you?'

'No, certainly not. We have not seen him.'

'Mr. Beecher,' she impatiently uttered, 'I asked you, at first, whether my husband had come here, and you said yes.'

'My dear young lady, I must have misunderstood you. All I heard, with reference to Captain Ordie, was, that he had come: I supposed to your house. He has certainly not been to ours.'

'Then what were you talking about?' she reproachfully asked of Mrs. Beecher. 'It was shameful to deceive me so! You said he had gone upstairs in slippers, and was finding his shoes. You know you did.'

'My dear child, I was speaking of Mr. Beecher. I did not know you thought your husband was here. Why did you think so?'

'If he is not here, where is he?' demanded Mrs. Ordie. 'You need not look at me as though you thought I was out of my senses. Do you mean to say you have not seen Captain Ordie?'

'We have not, indeed. We went to bed at ten, and heard nothing, until you threw the gravel at the window.'

'Where can he be? What can he have done with himself?'

'Did he leave you to come to us? When did he arrive?'

'It was at twenty-five minutes after eleven. I was sitting by baby, reading the *Vicar of Wakefield*. All at once I heard footsteps approaching from the upper gate, and I knew they were my husband's. I looked out, and saw him, and called to him; he did not seem to hear me, but went in to the portico. I ran down to let him in, and to my surprise he was not there, and I thought he must have come on to you.'

'Then you have not yet spoken with him?' exclaimed Mr. Beecher.

'Not yet.'

'Are you sure it was Captain Ordie? Who opened the gate to him?'

'No one. The gate is locked. There is the strange part of the business.'

'My dear Mrs. Ordie! I fear it must be all a mistake. Captain Ordie would not arrive here on foot, even if he landed unexpectedly; and he could not have got through a locked gate. Perhaps you were asleep.'

'Nonsense,' peevishly replied Mrs. Ordie; 'I was as wide awake as I am now. I had come to that part where the fine ladies from town had gone in to neighbour Flamborough's and caught them all at hunt-the-slipper, Olivia in the middle, bawling for fair play. The ballad "Edwin and Angelina" came in a few pages before, and that I skipped. I assure you I was perfectly awake.'

'I do not think it possible to have been anything but a delusion,' persisted Mr. Beecher.

'How a delusion?' angrily asked the young lady; 'I do not know what you mean. If my hearing could play me false, my sight could not. I heard my husband, and saw him, and spoke to him. He was in his regimentals: were they a delusion?'

'This is very strange,' said Mrs. Beecher. 'He would not be likely to travel in regimentals.'

'It is more than strange,' was Louisa Ordie's answer, as she looked dreamily about. 'He is in the grounds, somewhere, and why he does not come forward, I don't know.'

The mystery was not cleared up that night. No Captain Ordie made his appearance. The next day Mrs. Ordie sent for her father, to impart to him the strange circumstance. He adopted his curate's view of the affair; and, indeed, the universal view. Mrs. Ordie was much annoyed at their disbelief; and she actually, in spite of her friends, had Captain Ordie advertised for, in the local papers: he *was* in England, she said, and it would be proved so.

When letters next arrived from India, there was one from Captain Ordie, which gave proof positive that he was not, and had not been in Europe. Mrs. Ordie was perplexed.

The weeks went on, and the time fixed for the departure of Mrs. Ordie and her child drew near. But meanwhile the disastrous news had arrived of the outbreak in India of that dreadful mutiny, and it was deemed advisable to postpone it.

She was sitting one day in a gloomy mood. She had not heard from her husband for some time (his last letter was dated April); and now, as she found, another mail was in, and had brought no news from him. The rising at Delhi, where Captain Ordie was quartered, was known to her, but not, as yet, the details of its more disastrous features. She did not fear his having fallen: had anything happened to him, Mr. Main, or one of her sisters, would have written. They were all at Delhi.

As she thus sat, Mrs. Beecher came in, looking very pale

and sad. Dr. and Mrs. Ling had gone off in their pony-carriage to the county town, to pick up news. They were extremely uneasy.

'Another mail has been in these two days!' she exclaimed to Mrs. Beecher. 'News travels slower to Enton than anywhere. Have you heard from James Beecher? You don't look well.'

'James is come,' replied the curate's wife. 'He came overland.'

'And you have been worrying yourselves that he is dead!' retorted Louisa. 'How are things going on, over there?'

'Very badly. They cannot be worse.'

'Does he know anything of George?' continued she. 'I think he might spare just a minute from his fighting to write to me. What *is* the matter with you? You have not brought bad news for me?' she added, her fears touched, and rising in excitement. 'Oh, surely not! Not FOR ME!'

'James's news is altogether very dispiriting,' returned Mrs. Beecher, at a loss how to proceed with her task. 'My husband is gone to bring Dr. and Mrs. Ling back. We thought you might like them to be at home.'

'Has George fallen in battle? Have those half-caste rebels shot him down? Oh—'

'Pray be calm, Louisa!' implored Mrs. Beecher; 'if ever you had need of calmness in your life, you have need of it now.'

'Is he wounded? Is he dead?' interrupted Mrs. Ordie, with a bitter shriek. 'Oh, George! dearest George! and I have been calling you hard names for not writing to me! What is it?'

'There is a great deal to be told, my child. James Beecher was at Delhi in the midst of it.'

Louisa suddenly rose and flew from the room. Mrs.

Beecher, supposing she had gone to her chamber, went after her; but could not find her there. She had gone out of the house.

A thin man, looking fearfully ill, fair once, but browned by an Eastern sun, was lying on the sofa in the curate's parlour, when a young, excited woman came flying in.

'Mr. James Beecher,' she uttered, seizing his hands imploringly, 'when did it happen? I am Mrs. Ordie.'

'Has my sister-in-law told you – anything?' he hesitated.

'Yes, yes. I know the worst. I want particulars.'

He had risen into an upright posture, though he could scarcely support himself, and she sat down beside him. He was a church missionary, a widower with children. 'Are you sure that you can bear the details?' he asked, believing, from her words, that she knew the general facts.

'I am sure. Omit nothing. You were at Delhi.'

'I went there in the spring, to say farewell to some friends, ere I came home. At Delhi I was taken worse, and lay ill there.'

'But about the rising?'

'I am coming to it. On the second Monday in May, after breakfast, bad news came in. The 3rd Light Cavalry had dashed in from Meerut, fully armed, and were slaughtering the Europeans. Eighty-five of this regiment had been tried by court-martial at Meerut, for refusing to handle the greased cartridges, and sentenced to imprisonment. Their sentences were read out to them on parade on the previous Saturday, the 9th, and they were sent to gaol. On the 10th, Sunday, the regiment rose, released the prisoners, massacred the European officers, their wives and children, and on the 11th came to Delhi, in open revolt. I struggled up, dressed myself, joined the friends I was staying with, and we waited further news. It came in too soon. The mutineers had gone towards Deriowgunge, shooting all the officers they encountered. The brigadier ordered out the 54th Native Infantry and two guns; and I believe, a detachment of another regiment; but accounts varied. They met the rebels just outside the Cashmere gate, and it was all up, for the Sepoys deserted their officers, and shook hands with the Sowars. Every officer was killed. Treacherous, cowardly wretches! they did not spare one.'

She was biting her lips, and striving for calmness, determined to hear all. 'Did the officers make no resistance?'

'All that they could make, but they were unarmed,' he answered. 'The next account that came in was, that the natives had risen and joined the insurrection, were firing the bungalows at Deriowgunge, and ransacking the European residences. The troopers were raging about, destroying life; and when their work was done, the Goojours,* who had collected in great numbers, as they were sure to do, followed in their wake, and pillaged everything, even to the matting. The bank was rifled.'

Mr. Beecher paused, wondering whether he ought to proceed, but her studied calmness deceived him.

'No one knew where to fly for refuge, or what to do: none knew where to put the officers' wives and children. Many were taken to the Flagstaff Tower; but it was thought unsafe and had to be abandoned. Some escaped – many, I hope – in conveyances, or on horseback, or on foot. Some of the officers retreated to the cantonment outside the gates; but the troopers got there when night came, and killed them and their wives and children.'

---

* A race of a peculiar caste, who congregate round Meerut and Delhi. They have been compared to our gipsy tribes, and live by plunder, even in times of peace. Some years ago a regiment was obliged to be raised especially to keep them under.

'Were any of *my* family with them?' she asked, still with unnatural composure.

'No. I will tell you. Before mid-day, the ladies of our house, my host's wife and her cousin, escaped to a close hut, or outhouse, and I managed to hobble there with them. I don't know how I did it: but it is astonishing the artificial strength that fear brings out. Others also took refuge there, about half-a-dozen ladies, your two sisters being amongst them, three or four children, and a poor little ensign, as ill and weak as I was. We hoped we were in safety; that the rebels would not think of looking for us there; and some old matting, well wetted, was hung up across the entrance, as if to dry. A Sepoy, who was really faithful (and there were many such in the city), sat before it to guard it; many a one, raging after prey, did he turn aside with a well-assumed story that his old mother was in there, dying – let her die in peace.'

'Was my husband there?'

'Not then. No one came near us all that day: they dared not come, for our sakes; and we bore our suspense and apprehension as we best could, not knowing who was living or who dead, of those dearest to us. What a day that was! We had neither food nor drink; the heat of the weather was fearful; and so many of us stowed together, and closely shut up, rendered the air fetid. We thought it could not be less than a hundred and ten degrees. This was not the worst; there were apprehensions of discovery. We men might brave it, at any rate to appearance, but the poor young women! I believe they would have been glad to die as they cowered there, rather than live to encounter an uncertain fate. I strove to speak comfort to them all, but it was difficult; one or two bore bravely up, and cheered the rest. Late at night, under cover of the darkness, Captain Ordie stole in.'

She raised a faint cry at the name. 'My husband!'

'He told us what he could of the progress of the day – it was horribly bad, yet I believe he softened it for their ears – and then he began to talk of our own situation. It would be impossible, he said, to keep in the same place of concealment another day, and that we had better join a party who were about to make their escape towards Kurnaul. All seized at the idea eagerly, and wished to start without the delay of an instant. Mrs. Holt, my friend's wife, inquired after her husband, whom she had not seen since morning.

' "He is safe, and unharmed," replied Captain Ordie. "You will see him when we are fairly off; but it was not thought well for more than one of us to venture here."

' "And my husband?" added Mrs. Main, who had done nothing but clasp her baby to her breast all day, and weep silently. "Is he safe?" Captain Ordie answered evasively,' continued Mr. Beecher, 'and I knew, by his words and by the turn of his face, that poor Main was gone.'

'Go on,' groaned Mrs. Ordie. 'George's turn comes next.'

Mr. Beecher hesitated. 'I will finish later,' he suggested.

'No, finish now. You cannot leave me in this suspense. It would be cruel.'

'Captain Ordie spoke of the plan of departure. The officers had but three horses amongst them, and the ladies and invalids were to take it in turn to ride; two, with a child, on each horse. All the party were to keep together. At that moment arose a horrible yell, which we knew proceeded from a Sowar, and one of them appeared at the entrance, tearing down the matting. All the light we had was a nightwick in some oil, but we saw his dark face. The children shrieked; the ladies also, and huddled themselves together in a corner; and Captain Ordie advanced to the entrance, and dealt the man a blow on the temple with the butt-end of his pistol.'

'I hope it killed him!' she uttered, her eyes sparkling.

'I think it did, for he lay motionless. Captain Ordie kicked him out of the way, and, throwing himself on his hands and knees, crawled out cautiously to reconnoitre. Alas! we soon heard a struggle outside; two more were upon him.'

'And he was struck down! I *know* you are going to tell me so,' she uttered, in a low, passionate wailing.

Mr. Beecher sat silent, his countenance full of distress.

'Louisa, my darling, be composed,' interrupted Mrs. Beecher, who had come in search of her. 'You know the worst now.'

'Yes, I know the worst,' she moaned. 'They killed him, there and then.'

'They did,' whispered Mr. Beecher. 'It was instantaneous.'

She turned sick, and shook violently. But, by strong control, spoke again. 'Finish the history. What became of you, inside?'

'It was all commotion in a moment, dreadful commotion. The poor terrified women attempted to fly; some succeeded, and I hope escaped. Providentially there were only these two troopers; had more been upon us, none would have been left. The first thing I saw distinctly was, that one of them had caught Mrs. Main's infant, and was tossing it on the point of his bayonet. He next seized her.'

'Constance?' panted Mrs. Ordie.

'Yes. And killed her. Killed her instantly. Be thankful.'

Mrs. Ordie pressed down her eyelids, as if she would shut out some unwelcome sight. 'Constance murdered,' she moaned. 'And you tell me to be thankful!'

'Be ever thankful,' impressively spoke the missionary. 'Others met with a worse fate.'

'Sarah Ann?' she shivered. 'What became of her?'

'I am unable to tell you. I trust she escaped. At the moment of Mrs. Main's death, I fainted on the floor where I was lying, and that must have saved my life. When I recovered, not a creature – living – was to be seen. The children were lying about; they had been put out of their misery; two of the ladies, and the ensign. Poor young fellow! he had told us, in the day, that he had no parents or near friends to mourn him, so the loss of a little griff, if they did kill him, would not count for much.'

'Dead? All?'

'All. The two ladies were Mrs. Holt and Mrs. Main. Of the other ladies I saw no trace. I trust,' he added, clasping his hands fervently, 'that they escaped. We shall hear of many miraculous escapes: I pray that theirs may be of the number.'

'Now, Louisa, let me take you home,' urged Mrs. Beecher. 'You do know the worst.'

'I must hear all,' was the answer, uttered in a tone of frenzy. 'If I thought there was a word, a recital, left untold to me, I must get up in the middle of the night, and come and ask for it.'

'You have heard all,' said Mr. Beecher – 'all that I know. My own escape I will not trouble you with. It was wonderful: and I lost no time in coming home overland.'

She leaned back on the sofa and closed her eyes. Mrs. Beecher was thinking of her random words – that she would rather lose everything in the world than her child. But her thoughts had not grasped the dreadful possibility of losing her husband.

'When did this happen?' Mrs. Ordie suddenly asked. 'What date?'

'I mentioned it,' said Mr. Beecher. 'Late on the night of the 11th of May.'

She leaned forward breathless, her eyes staring. 'How late? The exact hour? Speak?'

'It must have been near half-past eleven. When Captain

Ordie came in, we asked him the time (for, strange to say, in our hurried flight, not one of us put a watch about us), and his watch said a quarter-past eleven; and we were talking, after that, perhaps ten minutes. It must have been about twenty-five minutes after eleven when he was killed.'

'Listen to that!' shrieked Louisa Ordie, seizing Mrs. Beecher by the arm. 'It was the very hour I saw and heard him. How was he dressed?' she rapidly asked.

'In full regimentals.'

'There! There! Do you believe me now, Mrs. Beecher? Ah! you all ridiculed me then; but you hear it! It was my husband that came down the path here – appearing to me in the moment of his death.'

The reader must judge of this mystery as he pleases. It happened; at least, to the positive belief of the lady, here called Mrs. Ordie; as her friends can testify. They reason with her in vain. They point out that twenty-five minutes after eleven in Delhi would not be twenty-five minutes after eleven here: they believe that it was, and could have been, nothing but her own vivid imagination, that her thoughts were probably running on her husband through the 'George' in the *Vicar of Wakefield*. But Louisa Ordie nevertheless believes, and will believe to the end of time, that it was her husband in the spirit who showed himself to her that unhappy night.

THE LADY ISOPEL

by Sir Gilbert Campbell

Sir Gilbert Edward Campbell, Bart, was one of the early champions of the newly-developing art of the detective story. He translated many French detective stories into English and published a volume of his own detective fiction in 1891. In addition he wrote plays, fairy tales for children and a series of admirable books of weird fiction including Dark Stories from the Sunny South *and* Wild and Weird, or, Remarkable Stories of Russian Life.

The Lady Isopel *is taken from his best work –* Mysteries of the Unseen, or, Supernatural Stories of English Life.

ONLY a few years have passed since the events which I have to narrate took place. They occurred in the spring-time of my youth, when all seemed bright and pleasant, whilst now, as I take the pen in my hand, and sit down to try and chronicle the sad events that blighted all my hopes, I feel what a wreck I am of my former self. Taking a portrait from a drawer in my writing-desk, and gazing upon the face of a fair young girl, over whose head nineteen summers had scarcely passed, I wonder if it can ever have been meant for me. What do I see? A face upon which care had never imprinted a line – a young, happy face, with dark sparkling eyes, and light-brown hair clustering over it in waving curls, and a mouth which seemed always breaking into a smile; whilst now, if I consult my mirror, it only shows me a face over which a deep sorrow has passed – the eyes are sunken and have lost all their fire, the mouth one which a smile can never hope to revisit, whilst the waving hair is thickly streaked with grey. Oh, what a change! and yet a little brief time and sorrow has worked all this.

I had been brought up all my life in the country, and except for an annual visit to the seaside with my governess, had never quitted my grandfather's house, Hardingham Hall. It was a quaint old place, that had been for many generations the seat of the Hardingham family, and though it had been added to and touched and retouched in different reigns, it still maintained its old characteristics of a Tudor manor house. The great entrance-gate was approached by a bridge which spanned a moat that encircled the building. Great care had been taken that the water in it should not become stagnant, and save where it was hidden by an abundant growth of water-lilies, it was as pure and silvery as a running stream. The great hall was a sight which once seen could never be forgotten, the black and white tesselated marble floor assumed strange hues as the moonbeams glinted through the coloured glass that filled the mullioned windows, and the suits of armour, antlered heads, and gleaming trophies of weapons with which the walls were adorned, seemed to be dyed a blood-red hue, as the last rays of the sun shone through the crimsoned panes. The wide staircase which led to the upper rooms was half shut off with faded velvet *portières*, which took strange and fantastic shapes as the wind, which always seemed to have ingress into the great hall, rolled itself into their folds, as though seeking for shelter there. A strange stillness hung over the whole place, only occasionally broken in the dark hours of the night by weird sounds, when the ancient woodwork creaked and groaned as though weary of having been confined in one place for so long a period, whilst the old servants seemed to have caught the infection of the house, and crept about the place as noiselessly as though they were shod with velvet. The only outward sign of life about the place was the lamp, which, as dusk came on, was always lighted in the north tower, where my grandfather spent the greater portion of his time perusing strange volumes of a curious description, the names of which are now almost forgotten, such as 'The Journey to the City of the Blue Distance', Anselm's 'Commentary upon the other Worlds', 'The Supernatural Life of Dietrich Von Löblh', and other works of a similar character.

I had no recollection of either father or mother: a fatal accident on the Lake of Geneva had deprived me of both parents at one fell blow, and my grandfather, though kind enough to me in his way, was so much taken up with his studies that I saw but little of him. And yet in that old dreamy house which seemed to sadden every one who resided in it, I grew up into a merry, laughing girl, and would move about its winding passages and quaint recesses at all hours without the slightest apprehension. Indoors I had my music, books, and painting to occupy my leisure hours, whilst in the gardens and stables I had flowers, and four-footed pets innumerable, so that time never hung heavily upon my hands. Of all my pets, however, only one was permitted to enter the house, and that one was my little fox-terrier Nip, who hardly ever left me, and always slept on a rug in my room. My first great sorrow was, I think, when my governess, Miss Halroyd, left me. Almost from the first I remembered her kind face near me, and when my grandfather decided that my studies were completed, and that I should assume my proper place as the future mistress of

Hardingham Hall, I thought that my heart would have broken at the separation. However, the feelings of youth are elastic, sorrow soon fades away, and though I did not forget my dear governess, and corresponded regularly with her, yet the wound that I had first felt at the separation was almost healed, the more so that my time was now fully taken up in superintending the household of the Hall. One bright summer's day, taking my book (and accompanied of course by Nip), I started for the woods that fringed the banks of the little river, the Lant, which bounds the Hardingham estate on the south side.

It was one of those delicious summer days which we often read of and seldom see, the shade in the woods was delightful, whilst beyond them the sun made the waters of the Lant look like a river of molten gold. The drowsy hum of the insects almost seemed to form itself into a kind of melody, and all nature appeared to be reposing during the heat of the day. I had been wandering through the woods plucking wild flowers, playing with Nip, and laughing at the fury with which he barked at the little squirrels, who watched him eagerly with their beady black eyes from their safe retreats in the old beech-trees, until, feeling tired, I sat down at the foot of a tree, and opening my book began to read.

I had not been occupied with it for more than a quarter of an hour when I heard a sharp yelp, followed by a succession of piteous whines; I started to my feet and looked round for Nip, but he was nowhere to be seen. I ran down to the river, and guided by the sound soon found my poor little dog. He had, I suppose, been in pursuit of a rat, and falling down the steep bank had rolled into the stream, where he had got so entangled in some of the weeds that he was unable to stir, and was beating the water with his forefeet and howling piteously. I did not know what to do. Nip was entirely beyond my reach, and I did not dare to venture into the stream to assist him. Poor dog, he was getting quite exhausted, his struggles were becoming more feeble every moment, and his whining fainter and fainter. I had almost given him up for lost when a gentleman suddenly made his appearance on the other side of the stream, and taking in the state of affairs at a glance waded into the water, and extricating Nip from his perilous position placed him at my feet.

'Miss Hardingham, I presume,' said he, raising his hat. 'We are neighbours, although we have never met. My name is Fenwick – Allan Fenwick. May I introduce myself?'

I knew the name at once. The Fenwick's estate adjoined ours, but though I had often met Colonel and Mrs. Fenwick, I had never before seen their son, who had been away doing duty with his regiment.

'Oh, Mr. Fenwick,' I said, extending my hand, 'I am sure no introduction is needed, for how can I thank you enough for saving my dog's life?'

'Not a very daring deed,' answered he, with a smile, 'I daresay that he would have extricated himself without my aid, only I thought it best to run no risks.'

'Ah, now you are making light of the great service you have rendered me,' said I, 'but you are dreadfully wet. Will you not come up to the Hall? – and I can send a man over for some dry things for you.'

'Thank you,' answered he, 'but it is not worth the trouble; I will just return as I came. But if you will permit me, I will call at the Hall when I am more in visiting trim than I am now,' and he pointed with a smile to the water that was streaming from his garments.

'I am sure I – that is, my grandfather – will be delighted to see you,' stammered I, as raising his hat he again waded through the stream and disappeared in the woods on the other side. And this was my first meeting with Allan Fenwick.

According to his promise, he very shortly after paid us a visit, and when once the ice was broken his calls were neither few nor far between; even my grandfather emerged from his seclusion and found pleasure in the society of a young man who could discuss with him his favourite studies.

And I – did I find pleasure in his company? As much as he did in mine, for it was the old story – Allan and I both learned to love each other, and as there were no obstacles to our union, with the mutual consent of my grandfather and Allan's parents we were engaged. It was, however, considered that we were both too young to incur the cares and responsibilities of married life, and therefore our marriage was arranged to take place in two years' time, during which Allan was to remain with his regiment. At the expiration of that period he was to sell out, we were to be married, and to take up our residence at Hardingham Hall. The parting between Allan and myself was a very sad one, though we hardly knew why we should feel it so much. His regiment was quartered in England; we had made every arrangement for a constant correspondence, and were both full of health and life; but for all that an unknown sorrow weighed down our hearts. At last, however, the dreaded parting was over, and for a few days I was absolutely prostrated; but youth will triumph sooner or later over sorrow, and after writing a letter of four pages to Allan, and receiving from him a reply full of love and tenderness, I began to feel better, and went about my customary avocations with a lighter heart. My grandfather had proposed to have the south wing of the Hall fitted up for us. This part of the building had been but little occupied of late, and had fallen into a rather dilapidated state. It was, however, one of my greatest pleasures to wander through the lonely rooms, and plan how they should be fitted up in that happy time when Allan and I should once more be together, never to be parted again. Sometimes in these rambles I took with me old Mrs. Meadows, who had been the housekeeper at the Hall for many years, and who was a perfect repository of all the old legends and stories of the Hardinghams. It was upon one of these excursions with her that I came to a door at the end of a long passage, which I had never noticed before. I tried the handle, but the door was locked.

'Mrs. Meadows,' said I, 'what is this room? I do not think that I have ever been into it.'

'Law, miss,' answered the old woman, 'that is the Lady Isopel's room; have you never heard of it?'

'Never!' exclaimed I. 'Have you got the key? Let us go in; and, above all, tell me who Lady Isopel was.'

'It is an uncanny room,' answered Mrs. Meadows, fumbling with a large bunch of keys which she carried, 'and I hardly think that you will do any good by going in, but still, I don't think that even she would do such a sweet child as you any harm.' And as she spoke she unlocked the door.

Full of curiosity, I pushed by her, and entered the room. The first thing that struck me was a faint odour of violets, the next the portrait of a woman hanging over the tall mantelpiece. Hers was a beautiful, but, at the same time, repulsive face; the features were regular and almost perfect, though the mouth was a little hard and cruel, but in the eyes there was a sinister light that was almost appalling, and marred all the beauty of the perfect features. I strove in vain to move my eyes from the picture; I was, as it were, fascinated, and it was not until the voice of Mrs. Meadows broke the spell that I was able to do so.

'Who is that awful-looking woman?' asked I, as soon as I could collect myself.

'That,' answered the housekeeper, 'is the Lady Isopel.'

'Yes; but who was she? Tell me all about her, dear Mrs. Meadows, for I am sure that there is some story connected with her,' said I, coaxingly.

'There is a story,' replied she, 'and not a very pretty one, either; but if you like I will tell you all I know about her. Lady Isopel was the wife of Gervase Hardingham, who lived in the reign of the blessed martyr, Charles I, and a bitter bad wife she was to him. When he was in arms, fighting like a loyal gentleman for the king, she was confiding all the secrets she had wormed out of him, affecting the royal cause, to a Roundhead captain whom she called her cousin. At last this man so worked upon her, that she agreed to give up the old Hall of which she had been left in charge to the Parliamentary troops, and at a certain hour they were to march up to the house and to take possession of it; but, somehow or other, her husband had heard of her treachery, and laid an ambush for the Roundheads some three miles from here, at a place they called Crosby Thicket. After a hard fight the cavaliers won the day, and Gervase slew the Puritan captain with his own hand; then, full of rage and fury, he rode on alone to tax the Lady Isopel with her treachery. He found her in this very room, dressed up in all her splendour, just taking a glance at herself in that old Venetian mirror, before going down to the great gate to meet her cousin. Bursting into the room he reproached her with her perfidy, and, drawing his sword, showed her the blood of her cousin still wet upon the blade. Until then she had listened to his taunts and reproaches in silence, but when she heard of her cousin's death, she uttered a loud shriek, and, turning upon her husband like a tigress, she told him that she loathed and hated him, that she had always loved her cousin, and would never cease to do so. "Nor," continued she, "will I survive him; but remember this, that when sorrow, misfortune, or disgrace come upon the Hardinghams—" "The latter can never come!" interrupted her husband, proudly. "It matters not," answered she. "But, mark me, when such times are coming, *I will be there*, and, before each calamity, I will show myself to those whom it will strike the heaviest. And now, farewell; but, ere I go, let me revenge the murder of my love," and, drawing a dagger from her bosom, she made so sudden a spring at her husband, that he had no time to defend himself, and the dagger, penetrating his throat just above the gorget, laid him dead upon the floor. Then, with another wild cry, she cast herself from the window, and it was not until the next day that her body was found floating in the moat.'

'What a terrible story,' said I, as Mrs. Meadows paused. 'And has she kept her word?'

'Yes,' replied she; 'and the last that saw her was your grandfather. He came into this room, I do not know why, and as he was gazing at the portrait he turned rapidly round and saw her, pale and indistinct, standing behind him with an arm raised as if to threaten him. That night,' continued Mrs. Meadows, lowering her voice, 'he heard of the sad accident to your poor father and mother.'

I felt inexpressibly shocked, and was anxious to get away from the fatal vicinity of the portrait as soon as possible, but an irresistible feeling prompted me to take a last look at it. The cruel mouth, the malignant glare of the eyes, the blue satin robe decorated with a bunch of violets, will remain for ever imprinted upon my memory. Suddenly, as I gazed, I felt a rush of cold air behind me; I turned quickly, and, as I live, I saw the Lady Isopel as plainly as if she had stepped out of her frame, standing behind me, with her arm raised menacingly. For a moment I saw her plainly, and then the vision passed away. With a faint cry I seized Mrs. Meadows by the arm and hurried her from the room. I would not reply to any of her questions, but only saying that

I felt faint, hastened away to my own chamber. On the table lay a letter in Allan's handwriting. I eagerly tore it open, and then sank back in my chair with a low cry. The Sikh war had broken out, and Allan's regiment had been ordered to proceed to the Punjab with as little delay as possible. I pass over my anguish. In my despair I had even urged on Allan to resign his commission, and it was only when he calmly laid before me the terrible consequences of his doing so when his regiment had been ordered upon active service, that I saw that I had nothing to do but to submit myself to my fate and to wait patiently, hoping for the best.

It was a very sad parting. Allan strove to cheer me up, and did his utmost to reassure me, but it was of little avail; the sad picture of his lying wounded and dying on the battlefield was ever before my eyes, and, do what I could, I was unable to tear from my mind the idea that the Lady Isopel had given her first warning of impending calamity.

Allan sailed, and a long period passed away without any news being received. I used to wander about the Hall like an unquiet spirit, picturing to myself the worst, and yet hoping that I might be mistaken. At last the sudden idea struck me that I would again visit the Lady Isopel's room; if I saw nothing, then Allan was safe, but if that terrible phantom again appeared, then at least I should be spared further suspense, and should know that Allan was lost to me for ever.

With some difficulty I obtained the key from Mrs. Meadows, and, rejecting her offer to attend me, I set out on my expedition, accompanied only by the faithful Nip.

I soon reached the door of the fatal chamber, and, as soon as I opened it, Nip bounded forward with a bark of joy, which, however, changed in a moment to a yelp of terror, as with his hair bristling and his eyes dilated, he rushed out again, and running to the end of the corridor, set up a terrible howl. For a moment my nerves were shaken, but, mustering up all my courage, I entered the room. The same faint odour of violets pervaded the atmosphere, and the portrait hung in its old place, with the same cruel light in its eyes; but I saw nothing more, and my spirits revived a little. I glanced around me, and my eye was caught by a Venetian hand mirror, in which, according to Mrs. Meadows' story, the ill-fated Lady Isopel had been gazing at herself at the moment of her husband's return. It was rather a large-sized hand-glass, set in a tortoiseshell frame, curiously inlaid with mother-of-pearl; mechanically retaining it in my hand, I glanced once more round the room, but, seeing nothing, I felt that all was yet safe, and closing the door of the chamber of fate, I rejoined Nip, who was still sitting at the end of the passage, uttering every now and then a low howl. Upon returning to my own room, I, for the first time, noticed that I had brought the Venetian mirror with me. I placed it upon my table, determining to restore it to its proper resting-place when next I visited (if I ever dared visit again) the Lady Isopel's chamber. That night I had a long talk with my grandfather over the Sutlej campaign. He had received news from a friend in the War Office, and had learned that as yet Allan was safe, and had not only escaped untouched, but had also been mentioned in despatches for gallantry in the field. This made me very happy, and for nearly a fortnight nothing occurred to ruffle my tranquil existence. At the end of that time my grandfather and I returned to the Hall about eleven o'clock at night, having been to dine with Colonel and Mrs. Fenwick. I wished my grandfather good-night and went up to my own room, or rooms, as I should more properly say, for I had two, a bedroom and a dressing-room, divided from each other by a green velvet curtain which hung in the doorway. I found Nip as usual lying upon his rug, and was received by him with every demonstration of friendship. Being very tired I lost no time in getting to bed, and must have fallen asleep almost immediately. How long I slept I do not know, but I was awoken by a fierce bark from Nip, and his rush through the curtain that divided the two rooms. In an instant his bark changed to a half-strangled howl, and then all was still. Trembling in every limb, I sat up in bed and listened intently. As I did so, a faint odour of violets seemed to pervade the room, and an unseen presence seemed to float around me and permeate my very soul. With a wild cry I clutched the bell-rope, and as I heard the answering clang, I fell back insensible. When I recovered it was broad daylight, and two of the women-servants were seated by my bedside. I felt weak and ill, but insisted upon dressing, as I was most desirous of speaking to my grandfather; but I found that he had gone over to Colonel Fenwick's, in compliance with a request contained in a note, which a mounted messenger had brought over. Having no alternative, then, but to await his return, I crept slowly downstairs, when, for the first time, I noticed the absence of Nip. Ringing the bell, I asked the butler what had become of my dog.

'Did you not know, miss?' replied he, with an air of surprise.

'Know what?' answered I. 'What do you mean?'

'That poor Nip is dead, miss. They have got him in the servants' hall; would you like to see him?'

My eyes filled with tears, as without further delay I made my way to the servants' quarters. There lay my poor Nip upon the great oaken table, quite dead; his mouth was half open, and his lips drawn back showed every fang, the hair upon his back and neck was still bristling up, and there was foam round his mouth.

'What did he die of?' asked I, as soon as my grief would allow me to speak.

'I don't know, miss,' replied Dulton, one of the keepers,

who happened to be in the room; 'but it looks to me just as if *he had died of fright.*'

Just then one of the grooms came in, and told me that my grandfather had returned, and would like to see me at once. I hastened to him, and as I entered the room saw that there was a deep shade upon his brow.

'My poor child,' said he, drawing me tenderly towards him, 'you have need of all your courage; bear up, things may not be as bad as they appear.'

'Quick! tell me all!' I cried; 'for pity's sake do not keep me any longer in suspense.'

'The Battle of Chillianwalla has been fought, and Allan's name has been returned to the lists as dangerously wounded,' replied he, in a low, grave tone.

Then I knew that the evil genius of our house had once more been with me, and could understand poor Nip's untimely end.

I am coming fast to the conclusion of my tale. A month of intense anxiety had passed away without our having received any reliable information from the seat of war regarding Allan. I had now nearly given up all hope, and passed my time in gloomy anticipations of misfortunes yet to come. One night after I had retired to bed, and had tossed about restlessly for some hours, I was startled by a slight sound in my dressing-room, as though some articles upon the toilet-table were being meddled with. Hardly knowing what I did I sprang from my bed, and partially drawing aside the curtain, I gazed into the dressing-room. As I did so I was again conscious of the well-remembered faint sweet perfume of violets. A figure in a blue satin dress was standing before the table gazing at itself in the Venetian mirror. A weird, unearthly phosphorescent light brought out every line and detail of its form in the sharpest relief. As I stared horror-struck at the apparition, it appeared to become conscious of my presence, and turned towards me. Never shall I forget the terrors of that face. The complexion seemed of a dull grey, through which the fierce eyes gleamed with a lambent flame, whilst the hard, cruel lips were half unclosed, showing a set of teeth, strong, sharp, and white as those of a young wolf. For a moment it gazed upon me, then with an expression of hideous malice it raised the hand that held the mirror, shook it at me with an air of savage menace, and then dashing the fragile toy into a thousand atoms at my feet, disappeared.

I did not faint this time, but I knew the worst. My maid, who slept in the adjoining room, startled by the crash of the broken glass, hurried in.

I gave her no explanation, but told her to dress me, and then, with the calmness of despair, sat down to await the news I expected, yet dreaded. It came all too soon – Allan Fenwick had died of his wounds!

What need to add more? They tell me that for months after the sad news I was delirious, and in my ravings only begged to be freed from a ghastly figure, that stood by my pillow, and that I cried wildly that I was being suffocated by violets. Perhaps she *was* standing by my couch during my illness – who knows? When I awoke to consciousness I had another loss to lament. The series of shocks had been too much for my poor old grandfather, and he had been found one morning cold and dead amongst his books. I am, and shall be, the last of the Hardinghams, for I shall never marry; and at my death the old Hall and the broad acres that belong to it, will pass away to the various charities to which I have willed it, and our name will no longer be known in the land.

THE WITCHES' SABBATH

by James Platt

Although, as we have seen, the influence of the Gothic School was seldom absent from the Victorian supernatural story, there was, in the eighteen-nineties, a notable, rather self-conscious revival of the Gothic tradition with Bram Stoker being the most successful (and durable) author to emerge. One of the most interesting works of this renaissance was Tales of the Supernatural, *published in 1893, from which this tale is taken. Its author, mediaeval scholar and self-taught philologist James Platt (1861–1910), was among the compilers of the* Oxford English Dictionary *and, incidentally, contributed a well-informed survey of London's opium dens to the* Gentleman's Magazine.

A contemporary critic remarked that Tales of the Supernatural *was a work to which the 'author has brought the force of expression and fire of imagination of the poet as well as the patient research of the scholar'.*

OUR scene is one of those terrific peaks set apart by tradition as the trysting place of wizards and witches, and of every kind of folk that prefers dark to day.

It might have been Mount Elias, or the Brocken, associated with Doctor Faustus. It might have been the Horsel or

Venusberg of Tannhaeuser, or the Black Forest. Enough that it was one of these.

Not a star wrinkled the brow of night. Only in the distance the twinkling lights of some town could be seen. Low down in the skirts of the mountain rode a knight, followed closely by his page. We say a knight, because he had once owned that distinction. But a wild and bloody youth had tarnished his ancient shield, the while it kept bright and busy his ancestral sword. Behold him now, little better than a highwayman. Latterly he had wandered from border to border, without finding where to rest his faithful steed. All authority was in arms against him; Hageck, the wild knight, was posted throughout Germany. More money was set upon his head than had ever been put into his pocket. Pikemen and pistoliers had dispersed his following. None remained to him whom he could call his own, save this stripling who still rode sturdily at the tail of his horse. Him also, the outlaw had besought, even with tears, to abandon one so ostensibly cursed by stars and men. But in vain. The boy protested that he would have no home, save in his master's shadow.

They were an ill-assorted pair. The leader was all war-worn and weather-worn. Sin had marked him for its own and for the wages of sin. The page was young and slight, and marble pale. He would have looked more at home at the silken train of some great lady, than following at these heels from which the gilded spurs had long been hacked. Nevertheless, the music of the spheres themselves sings not more sweetly in accord than did these two hearts.

The wild knight, Hageck, had ascended the mountain as far as was possible to four-legged roadsters. Therefore he reined in his horse and dismounted, and addressed his companion. His voice was quite gentle, which on occasion could quench mutiny, and in due season dry up the taste of blood in the mouths of desperate men.

'Time is that we must part, Enno.'

'Master, you told me we need never part.'

'Let be, child, do you not understand me? I hope with your own heart's hope that we shall meet again tomorrow in this same tarrying place. But I have not brought you to so cursed a place without some object. When I say that we must part, I mean that you must take charge of our horses while I go further up the mountain upon business, which for your own sake you must never share.'

'And is this your reading of the oath of our brotherhood which we swore together?'

'The oath of our brotherhood, I fear, was writ in water. You are, in fact, the only one of all my company that has kept faith with me. For that very reason I would not spare your neck from the halter, nor your limbs from the wheel. But also for that very reason I will not set your immortal soul in jeopardy.'

'My immortal soul! Is this business then unhallowed that you go upon? Now I remember me that this mountain at certain seasons is said to be haunted by evil spirits. Master, you also are bound by our oath to tell me all.'

'You shall know all, Enno, were oaths even cheaper than they are. You have deserved by your devotion to be the confessor of your friend.'

'Friend is no name for companionship such as ours. I am sure you would die for me. I believe I could die for you, Hageck.'

'Enough, you have been more than brother to me. I had a brother once, after the fashion of this world, and it is his envious hand which has placed me where I stand. That was before I knew you, Enno, and it is some sweets in my cup at any rate, that had he not betrayed me I should never have known you. Nevertheless, you will admit that since he robbed me of the girl I loved, even your loyal heart is a poor set off for what fate and fraternity took from me. In fine, we both loved the same girl, but she loved me, and would have none of my brother. She was beautiful, Enno – how beautiful you can never guess that have not yet loved.'

'I have never conceived any other love than that I bear you.'

'Tush, boy, you know not what you say. But to return to my story. One day that I was walking with her my brother would have stabbed me. She threw herself between and was killed upon my breast.'

He tore open his clothes at the throat and showed a great faded stain upon his skin.

'The hangman's brand shall fade,' he cried, 'ere that wash out. Accursed be the mother that bore me seeing that she also first bore him! The devil squat down with him in his resting, lie with him in his sleeping, as the devil has sat and slept with me every noon and night since that deed was done. Never give way to love of woman, Enno, lest you lose the one you love, and with her lose the balance of your life.'

'Alas! Hageck, I fear I never shall.'

'Since that miscalled day, blacker than any night, you know as well as anyone the sort of death in life I led. I had the good or evil luck to fall in with some broken men like myself, fortune's foes and foes of all whom fortune cherishes, you among them. Red blood, red gold for a while ran through our fingers. Then a turn of the wheel, and, presto, my men are squandered to every wind that blows – I am a fugitive with a price upon my head!'

'And with one comrade whom, believe me, wealth is too poor to buy.'

'A heart above rubies. Even so. To such alone would I confide my present purpose. You must know that my brother was a student of magic of no mean repute, and before we quarrelled had given me some insight into its mysteries. Now that I near the end of my tether I have summed up all the little I knew, and am resolved to make a desperate cast in this mountain of despair. In a word, I intend to hold converse with my dead sweetheart before I die. The devil shall help me to it for the love he bears me.'

'You would invoke the enemy of all mankind?'

'Him and none other. Aye, shudder not, nor seek to turn me from it. I have gone over it again and again. The gates of Hell are set no firmer than this resolve.'

'God keep Hell far from you when you call it!'

'I had feared my science was of too elementary an order to conduct an exorcism under any but the most favourable circumstances. Hence our journey hither. This place is one of those where parliaments of evil are held, where dead and living meet on equal ground. To-night is the appointed night of one of these great Sabbaths. I propose to leave you here with the horses. I shall climb to the topmost peak, draw a circle that I may stand in for my defence, and with all the vehemence of love deferred, pray for my desire.'

'May all good angels speed you!'

'Nay, I have broken with such. Your good wish, Enno, is enough.'

'But did we not hear talk in the town about a hermit that spent his life upon the mountain top, atoning for some sin in day-long prayer and mortification? Can this evil fellowship of which you speak still hold its meetings upon a spot which has been attached in the name of Heaven by one good man?'

'Of this hermit I knew nothing until we reached the town. It was then too late to seek another workshop. Should what you say be correct, and this holy man have purged this plague spot, I can do no worse than pass the night with him, and return to you. But should the practices of witch and wizard continue as of yore, then the powers of evil shall draw my love to me, be she where she may. Aye, be it in that most secret nook of heaven where God retires when He would weep, and where even archangels are never suffered to tread.'

'O all good go with you!'

'Farewell, Enno, and if I never return count my soul not so lost but what you may say a prayer for it now and again, when you have leisure.'

'I will not outlive you!'

The passionate words were lost on Hageck, who had already climbed so far as to be out of hearing. He only knew vaguely that something was shouted to him, and waved his hand above his head for a reply. On and on he climbed. Time passed. The way grew harder. At last exhausted, but fed with inward exaltation, he reached the summit. It was of considerable extent and extremely uneven. The first thing our hero noticed was the cave of the hermit. It could be nothing else, although it was closed with an iron door. A new departure, thought Hageck to himself, as he hammered upon it with the pommel of his sword, for a hermit's cell to be locked in like a fortress.

'Open, friend,' he cried, 'in heaven's name, or in that of the other place if you like it better.'

The noise came from within of a bar being removed. The door opened. It revealed a mere hole in the rock, though large enough, it is true, to hold a considerable number of persons. Furniture was conspicuous by its absence. There was no sign even of a bed, unless a coffin that grinned in one corner served the occupant's needs. A skull, a scourge, a crucifix, a knife for his food, what more does such a hermit want? His feet were bare, his head was tonsured, but his eyebrows were long and matted, and fell like a screen over burning maniacal eyes. A fanatic, every inch of him. He scrutinized the invader from top to toe. Apparently the result was unsatisfactory. He frowned.

'A traveller,' said he, 'and at this unholy hour. Back, back, do you not know the sinister reputation of this time and place?'

'I know your reputation to be of the highest, reverend father; I could not credit what rumour circulates about this mountain top when I understood that one of such sanctity had taken up a perpetual abode here.'

'My abode is fixed here for the very reason that it is a realm of untold horror. My task is to win back, if I can, to the dominion of the church this corner, which has been so long unloved that it cries aloud to God and man. This position of my own choice is no sinecure. Hither at stated times the full brunt of the Sabbath sweeps to its rendezvous. Here I defy the Sabbath. You see that mighty door?'

'I had wondered, but feared to ask, what purpose such a barrier could serve in such a miserable place.'

'You may be glad to crouch behind it if you stay here much longer. At midnight, Legion, with all the swirl of all the hells at his back, will sweep this summit like a tornado. Were you of the stuff that never trembles, yet you shall hear such sounds as shall melt your backbone. Avoid hence while there is yet time.'

'But you, if you remain here, why not I?'

'I remain here as a penance for a crime I did, a crime which almost takes prisoner my reason, so different was it from the crime I set out to do, so deadly death to all my hopes. I am on my knees throughout the whole duration of this pandemonium that I tell you of, and count thick and fast my beads during the whole time. Did I cease for one second to pray, that second would be my last. The roof of my cavern would descend and efface body and soul. But you, what would you do here?'

'I seek my own ends, for which I am fully prepared. To confer with a shade from the other world I place my own soul in jeopardy. For the short time that must elapse, before the hour arrives when I can work, I ask but a trifle of your light and fire.'

'The will-o'-the-wisp be your light, Saint Anthony's your fire! Do you not recognize me?'

The wild knight bent forward and gazed into the hermit's inmost eye, then started back, and would have fallen had his head not struck the iron door. This recalled him to his senses, and after a moment he stood firm again, and murmured between his teeth, 'My brother!'

'Your brother,' repeated the holy man, 'your brother, whose sweetheart you stole and drove me to madness and crime.'

'I drove you to no madness, I drove you to no crime. The madness, the crime you expiate here, were all of your own making. She loved me, and me alone – you shed her blood, by accident I confess, yet you shed it, and not all the prayers of your lifetime can gather up one drop of it. What soaked into my own brain remains there for ever, though I have sought to wash it out with an ocean of other men's blood.'

'And I,' replied the hermit, and he tore his coarse frock off his shoulders, 'I have sought to drown it with an ocean of my own.'

He spoke truth. Blood still oozed from his naked flesh, ploughed into furrows by the scourge.

'You, that have committed so many murders,' he continued, 'and who have reproached me so bitterly for one, all the curses of your dying victims, all the curses I showered upon you before I became reformed have not availed to send you yet to the gibbet or to the wheel. You are one that, like the basil plant, grows ever the rifer for cursing. I remember I tried to lame you, after you left home, by driving a rusty nail into one of your footsteps, but the charm refused to work. You were never the worse for it that I could hear. They say the devil's children have the devil's luck. Yet some day shall death trip up your heels.'

'Peace, peace,' cried the wild horseman, 'let ill-will be dead between us, and the bitterness of death be passed, as befits your sacred calling. Even if I see her for one moment to-night, by the aid of the science you once taught me, will you not see her for eternity in heaven some near day?'

'In heaven,' cried the hermit, 'do I want to see her in heaven? On earth would I gladly see her again and account that moment cheap if weighed against my newly discovered soul! But that can never be. Not the art you speak of, not all the dark powers which move men to sin, can restore her to either of us as she was that day. And she loved you. She died to save you. You have nothing to complain of. But to me she was like some chaste impossible star.'

'I loved her most,' muttered the outlaw.

'You loved her most,' screamed the hermit. 'Hell sit upon your eyes! Put it to the test. Look around. Do you see anything of her here?'

The other Hageck gazed eagerly round the cave, but without fixing upon anything.

'I see nothing,' he was forced to confess.

The hermit seized the skull and held it in front of his eyes.

'This is her dead head,' he cried, 'fairer far than living red and white to me!'

The wild knight recoiled with a gasp of horror, snatched the ghastly relic from the hand of his brother, and hurled it over the precipice. He put his fingers over his eyes and fell to shaking like an aspen. For a moment the hermit scarcely seemed to grasp his loss. Then with a howl of rage he seized his brother by the throat.

'You have murdered her,' he shrieked in tones scarcely

recognizable, 'she will be dashed to a hundred pieces by such a fall!'

He threw the outlaw to the ground and, retreating to his cave, slammed the door behind him, but his heart-broken sobs could still be heard distinctly. It was very evident that he was no longer in his right mind. The wild knight rose somewhat painfully and limped to a little distance where he perceived a favourable spot for erecting his circle. The sobbing of the crazed hermit presently ceased. He was aware that his rival had entered upon his operations. The hermit re-opened his door that he might more clearly catch the sound of what his foe was engaged upon. Every step was of as absorbing interest to the solitary as to the man who made it. Anon the hermit started to his feet. He fancied he heard another voice replying to his brother. Yes, it was a voice he seemed to know. He rushed out of the cave. A girlish figure clad in a stained dress was clasped in his brother's arms. Kiss after kiss the wild knight was showering upon brow, and eye, and cheek, and lip. The girl responded as the hermit had surely seen her do once before. He flew to his cave. He grasped the knife he used for his food. He darted like an arrow upon the startled pair. The woman tried to throw herself in front of her lover, but the hermit with a coarse laugh, 'Not twice the dagger seeks the same breast,' plunged it into the heart of her companion. The wild knight threw up his arms and without a cry fell to the ground. The girl uttered a shriek that seemed to rive the skies and flung herself across her dead lovers body. The hermit gazed at it stupidly and rubbed his eyes. He seemed like one dazed, but slowly recovering his senses. Suddenly he started, came as it were to himself, and pulled the girl by the shoulder.

'We have not a minute to lose,' he cried, 'the great Sabbath is all but due. If his body remains out here one second after the stroke of twelve, his soul will be lost to all eternity.

It will be snatched by the fiends who even now are bound to it. Do you not see yon shadowy hosts – but I forget, you are not a witch.'

'I see nothing,' she replied, sullenly, rising up and peering round. The night was clear, but starless.

'I have been a wizard,' he answered, 'and once a wizard always a wizard, though I now fight upon the other side. Take my hand and you will see.'

She took his hand, and screamed as she did so. For at the instant there became visible to her those clouds of loathsome beings that were speeding thither from every point of the compass. Warlock, and witch, and wizard rode past on every conceivable graceless mount. Their motion was like the lightning of heaven, and their varied cries – owlet hoot, caterwaul, dragon-shout – the horn of the Wild Hunter, and the hurly of risen dead – vied with the bay of Cerberus to the seldseen moon. A forest of whips was flourished aloft. The whirr of wings raised dozing echoes. The accustomed mountain shook and shivered like a jelly, with the fear of their onset.

The girl dropped his hand and immediately lost the power of seeing them. She had learned at any rate that what he said was true.

'Help me to carry the body to the cave,' cried he, and in a moment it was done. The corpse was placed in the coffin of his murderer. Then the hermit crashed his door to its place. Up went bolts and bars. Some loose rocks that were probably the hermit's chairs and tables were rolled up to afford additional security.

'And now,' demanded the man, 'now that we have a moment of breathing space, tell me what woman-kind are you whom I find here with my brother? That you are not her I know (woe is me that I have good reason to know) yet you are as like her as any flower that blows. I loved her, and

I murdered her, and I have the right to ask, who and what are you that come to disturb my peace?'

'I am her sister.'

'Her sister! Yes, I remember you. You were a child in those days. Neither I nor my brother (God rest his soul!), neither of us noticed you.'

'No, he never took much notice of me. Yet I loved him as well as she did.'

'You, too, loved him,' whispered the hermit, as if to himself; 'what did he do to be loved by two such women?'

'Yes, I loved him, though he never knew it, but I may confess it now, for you are a priest of a sort, are you not, you that shrive with steel?'

'You are bitter, like your sister. She was always so with me.'

'I owe you my story,' she replied more gently; 'when she died and he fell into evil courses and went adrift with bad companions, I found I could not live without him, nor with anyone else, and I determined to become one of them. I dressed in boy's clothes and sought enlistment into his company of free lances. He would have driven me from him, saying it was no work for such as I, yet at last I wheedled it from him. I think there was something in my face (all undeveloped as it was and stained with walnut juice) that reminded him of her he had lost. I followed him faithfully through good and evil, cringing for a look or word from him. We were at last broken up (as you know) and I alone of all his sworn riders remained to staunch his wounds. He brought me hither that he might wager all the soul that was left to him on the chance of evoking her spirit. I had with me the dress my sister died in, that I had cherished through all my wanderings, as my sole reminder of her life and death. I put it on after he had left me, and followed him as fast as my strength would allow me. My object was to beguile him with what sorry pleasure I could, while at the same time saving him from committing the sin of disturbing the dead. God forgive me if there was mixed with it the wholly selfish yearning to be kissed by him once, only once, in my true character as loving woman, rid of my hated disguise! I have had my desire, and it has turned to apples of Sodom on my lips. You are right. All we can do now is to preserve his soul alive.'

She fell on her knees beside the coffin. The hermit pressed his crucifix into her hands.

'Pray!' he cried, and at the same moment the distant clock struck twelve. There came a rush of feet, a thunder at the iron door, the cave rocked like a ship's cabin abruptly launched into the trough of a storm. An infernal whooping and hallooing filled the air outside, mixed with its imprecations that made the strong man blanch. The banner of Destruction was unfurled. All the horned heads were upon them. Thrones and Dominions, Virtues, Princes, Powers. All hell was loose that night, and the outskirts of Hell.

The siege had begun. The hermit told his beads with feverish rapidity. One Latin prayer after another rolled off his tongue in drops of sweat. The girl, to whom these were unintelligible, tried in vain to think of prayers. All she could say, as she pressed the Christ to her lips, was 'Lord of my life! My Love.' She scarcely heard the hurly-burly that raged outside. Crash after crash resounded against the door, but good steel tempered with holy water is bad to beat. Showers of small pieces of rock fell from the ceiling and the cave was soon filled with dust. Peals of hellish cachinnation resounded after each unsuccessful attempt to break down that defence. Living battering rams pressed it hard, dragon's spur, serpent's coil, cloven hoof, foot of clay. Tall Iniquities set their backs to it, names of terror, girt with earthquake. All the swart crew dashed their huge bulk against it, rakehelly riders, humans and superhumans, sin and its paymasters. The winds well nigh split their sides with hounding of them on. Evil stars in their courses fought against it. The seas threw up their dead. Haunted houses were no more haunted that night. Graveyards steamed. Gibbets were empty. The ghoul left his half-gnawn corpse, the vampire his victim's throat. Buried treasures rose to earth's surface that their ghostly guardians might swell the fray. Yet the hermit prayed on, and the woman wept, and the door kept its face to the foe. Will the hour of release never strike? Crested Satans now lead the van. Even steel cannot hold out for ever against those in whose veins instead of blood, runs fire. At last it bends ever so little, and the devilish hubbub is increased tenfold.

'Should they break down the door—' yelled the hermit, making a trumpet of his hands, yet she could not hear what he shouted above the abominable din, nor had he time to complete his instructions. For the door did give, and that suddenly, with a clang that was heard from far off in the town, and made many a burgher think the last trump had come. The rocks that had been rolled against the door flew off in every direction, and a surging host – and the horror of it was that they were invisible to the girl – swept in.

The hermit tore his rosary asunder, and scattered the loose beads in the faces of the fiends.

'Hold fast the corpse!' he yelled, as he was trampled under foot, and this time he made himself heard. The girl seized the long hair of her lover, pressed it convulsively, and swooned.

Years afterwards (as it seemed to her) she awakened and found the chamber still as death, and – yes – this was the hair of death which she still clutched in her dead hand. She kissed it a hundred times before it brought back to her where she was and what had passed. She looked round then for the hermit. He, poor man, was lying as if also dead. But when she could bring herself to release her hoarded treasure, she speedily brought him to some sort of consciousness. He sat up, not without difficulty, and looked around. But his mind, already half-way to madness, had been totally overturned by what had occurred that woeful night.

'We have saved his soul between us,' she cried. 'What do I not owe you for standing by me in that fell hour?'

He regarded her in evident perplexity. 'I cannot think how you come to be wearing that blood-stained dress of hers,' was all he replied.

'I have told you,' she said, gently, 'but you have forgotten that I cherished it through all my wanderings as my sole memento of her glorious death. She laid down the last drop of her blood for him. She chose the better part. But I! my God! what in the world is to become of me?'

'I had a memento of her once,' he muttered. 'I had her beautiful head, but I have lost it.'

'That settles it,' she said, 'you shall cut off mine.'

THE SKELETON HAND

by Agnes MacLeod

A chaste tragic heroine; a black-hearted scoundrel; divine retribution and a stiff dose of moralizing: the mixture is unmistakably Victorian. The Skeleton Hand *has them all but here the effect is far from dismal.*

The writer of the story, which appeared in Blackwood's *for October, 1894, was Lady Agnes MacLeod, wife of Sir Reginald MacLeod. As far as I have been able to discover it is, unfortunately, her only published work of fiction. She died in 1921.*

I AM about to relate some events which took place in the early part of this century, in a remote little fishing village on the south coast of Devonshire. The occurrences are themselves so remarkable that they have been well known to the present generation of inhabitants; but as things get altered in oral transmission through many persons, it has been thought well to place this record in writing.

Near the village of Jodziel, in a pretty little cottage on the top of the bright red sandstone cliff which overhangs the village, lived two maiden sisters, the Misses Rutson. Their father, a sea-captain, had died a year before the events I am about to relate occurred. Their mother had died in giving birth to the younger sister, Anne, who was now a most beautiful girl of eighteen. The Misses Rutson were very devotedly attached to one another, and were much beloved by the village neighbours. The hamlet being a very sequestered one, they seldom saw any one from the outer world except occasionally sailors, who would stroll along the cliff from Plymouth or from other fishing villages along the coast. In the autumn of 1813 a pressgang visited South Devon and made their headquarters for some time in the village of Jodziel. The captain, a certain Captain Sinclair by name – a coarse brutal fellow in appearance – was very much struck by the extraordinary beauty of Miss Anne. He forced himself upon her, and continued paying her the most distasteful attentions, which the gentle girl did her very utmost to check, but in vain. The day before Captain Sinclair left Jodziel, he made a formal offer of marriage to Miss Anne, which in the presence of her sister she immediately and decisively declined. Captain Sinclair flew into the most violent passion, swore he had never been thwarted yet by any woman, and that she should belong to him or never marry at all. Anne was so much upset by the terrible scene, and by Captain Sinclair's outrageous language, that her sister was very glad when an invitation from an aunt residing in London gave Anne a few weeks' much-needed change. Mrs. Travers was the only near relative remaining to the Misses Rutson, and owing to various circumstances the sisters had seen but little of their aunt, though with Maurice Travers, her only son, they were better acquainted. Maurice's regiment had been quartered for the summer of 1813 at Plymouth, and he had frequently been over to see his cousins, and many a pleasant summer day had they spent wandering along the beautiful Devonshire coast. Miss Rutson had not been slow to perceive that stronger attractions than those of mere scenery brought the young officer so constantly to their cottage, and she was not therefore very much surprised at receiving one morning, about three weeks after Anne's departure from home, a letter announcing her engagement to her cousin, Maurice Travers, and her immediate return to Jodziel. It was decided that the marriage should take place early in the following May, and I will now quote one or two passages from Miss Rutson's diary at this time.

'*May 1*. – Such a horrid meeting we have just had. Anne and I had been for a stroll along the shore when we noticed a little boat which lay drawn up under a rock at some distance, and Anne's eyes, which are keener than mine, caught sight of the name painted in gold letters. "Ah, sister, come away," she cried; "it is a boat from the Raven. I thought Captain Sinclair was not to be in these waters again; he told me he was to sail for the West Indies last month." We turned, and were hurriedly retracing our steps towards the house when we heard a cry of *Stop*! I looked at Anne; she was deadly white. "Run on quick," I cried; "I will speak to him." My heart was beating so fast I could run no longer; besides, I felt it might be well to hear what Captain Sinclair had to say, so I drew myself together and waited. Presently he appeared clambering up the side of the cliff, his swarthy face purple with excitement. "Where is she?" he gasped. "I have come back to fetch her; I could not sail without her, my own beautiful Anne!" "Recollect yourself, sir," I cried indignantly. "How dare you speak of my sister in this free manner! She has told you most clearly, and that in my presence, that she looks on your pursuit of her as odious, and she begs, both for her own sake and yours, that you will never attempt to see her again." "Do you think I will be daunted by such a speech from a foolish girl?" he answered scornfully; "No, no, she shall be mine yet, whether she will or no." "You are mistaken," I replied as calmly as I could; "Next Monday she marries our first cousin, Maurice

Travers, and will be at peace from your hated persecutions."

'I shall never forget his scowl of fury as he turned from me and dashed down the cliff, shouting as he did so, "She shall be mine!" When I got home, feeling very nervous and shaken, who should I find just starting out to seek me but Maurice, who had come three days earlier than we expected him. An hour before I should have felt very cross at having my last quiet hours with Anne so much curtailed, but now I was only too thankful to feel we had a protector near us. He went out after hearing my story, but could see no trace of either boat or its owner.

'*May 2.* – To my great relief the Raven, with Captain Sinclair on board, has left Plymouth this morning for the West Indies. Maurice had business at Plymouth, and he took the opportunity of making inquiries concerning the Raven, which was, he found, in the very act of putting to sea. I feel, oh, so thankful and relieved.

'*May 4.* – How shall I ever begin to write the events of this most dreadful day! Such a brilliant sunshiny morning, quite like summer, and my darling came down looking like one of the sweet white roses which were just coming into bloom around the windows. I plucked a beautiful spray of them, and she put them in her white satin waistband just before starting for church. I have those roses by me now as I write, but, O my darling! where are you? The wedding was a very quiet one. After the ceremony we had the clergyman and doctor, with their wives and their children, to lunch, and presently Anne rose and said she would go and change her dress. I was going to follow her, but she stopped me with one of her sweet kisses and said, "Let me have a few moments alone in the old room to say good-bye to it all." I let her go – when did I ever thwart her in anything? She went, and Maurice began romping with the children, and we ladies cut slices of wedding-cake, to be taken round to village favourites next day, and still Anne did not call. Once, indeed, I had fancied I heard her voice; but when I had gone upstairs her door was locked, and she had not answered my gentle tap, so I came down again, not wishing to intrude upon her privacy. At length, however, Maurice became impatient, and said I must go and fetch her down, or they would never be in time to catch the coach at Plymouth. The door was still locked. When I got upstairs I knocked, first gently, then more loudly. I was not frightened at first, for there was a door-window in the room leading down a little flight of steps into the garden, and I thought she had gone down these to take a last look at her flowers, so I called to Maurice to run round to the garden, for she must be there. I remained listening at the bedroom door, which in a moment or two flew open, and Maurice, with a very disturbed face, stood before me. "She has evidently been in the garden," he said, "for the door on to the outside steps was open; but there is no one there now." I made no answer, but flew past him into the bedroom. It needed but a glance to show my darling had gone straight through the room; her gloves and handkerchief were thrown on a chair by the window, and her pale-blue travelling-dress lay undisturbed upon the bed. I ran hastily through the room and garden, which was empty; the gate on to the cliff was ajar, and we noticed (but not till later) that there must have been a struggle at the spot, for some of the lilac boughs were torn down, as if someone had held fast by them and been dragged forcibly away. Maurice and the rest of the party followed me on to the cliff, for the alarm had now become general; for a little while we ran wildly, calling her dear name, but presently Maurice came to me, and drawing my arm within his own, led me back towards the house. "Someone must be here to receive her when she comes home," he said gently, and here his lips grew white. "It might be well to have her bed ready in case—" He was out of the room without finishing his sentence. It was needless; the same horrible fear had already seized on me. The cliff, the terrible cliff; I cannot go on writing, my heart is too heavy.

'*Twelve o'clock.* – They have come back, and, O God! the only trace of her is the spray of white roses I picked for her this morning. They were found on top of the cliff about half a mile from here. I think they are a message from my darling to me, for they were not trampled on or crushed; she must have taken them carefully and purposely from her belt; they shall never, never leave me.

'*May 11.* – It is a week since that dreadful day, and not the smallest clue to her disappearance. Poor Maurice is half mad with grief; he has sought for her high and low, and spent all the little sum destined for their wedding journey on these vain researches. Now he wanders along the cliff up and down, up and down, the whole of the long day, and then he comes and sits opposite to me with his elbows on his knees, till I tell him it is time for bed, when he goes without a word; but I hear him pacing his room half the night.

'*May 31.* – Maurice has had to join his regiment for foreign service. I am glad: he would have gone mad had he remained inactive here.

'*Sept. 3.* – I have been very ill, but Patty assures me there has not been a trace of any clue during my long time of blessed unconsciousness, and now the terrible aching void is again here. O my darling, my darling, come back!

'*Sept. 6.* – Why should I go on writing? my life henceforth is only waiting.'

After this comes a long break of fully twenty years in the diary; then in an aged and trembling character occurs the following entry:

'*May 4, 1835.* – I don't know, what impels me once more to pen this diary; possibly this wild hurricane of wind which is making the house rock like a boat has upset me, but I feel so glad and satisfied, as if my long waiting were nearly over. I have just been upstairs to see that all is in order for my darling. We have kept everything aired and prepared for her these thirty years, so that she should find all comfortable when she comes home at last. My poor darling, she will only find Patty and me to welcome her. Let me think, this is nearly twenty years ago since we heard of Maurice's death at Waterloo. Oh what a fearful crash! and how that rumbling noise goes on sounding as if the cliff had given way.'

Here the diary abruptly terminates; but the remainder of the tragic story is yet told in that little Devonshire village. The violence of the storm had in very truth caused a subsidence in the cliff, and in doing so had brought to light a skeleton on which yet hung some tattered remnants of what had once been white satin, and from whose bony fingers rolled a tarnished wedding-ring. The bones were collected with tender care and brought to the house of the unhappy sister. She received them without much apparent surprise, directed they should be laid on 'Miss Anne's bed upstairs,' and as soon as the men had left the house, went and laid herself upon the bed also, where her faithful maid Patty, coming to see after her an hour later, found her stone-dead, and held tight in her dead grasp was a pair of white gloves and a lace pocket-handkerchief.

The two sisters were laid to rest in one grave, and it was not till after the funeral was over that it was discovered that, through some inadvertence, one of the skeleton hands had not been placed in the coffin with the rest of the body.

At first there was some talk of reopening the grave, but the old maid Patty entreated so earnestly to be allowed to retain the hand that she at last succeeded in carrying her point. A glass case was made by Mrs. Patty's order, and in it the poor hand was placed; and when Mrs. Patty went down to the inn to spend her last remaining years with her daughter the landlady, the case was placed on a shelf close to the old woman's seat, and many a time would she recount the sad story to the sailors who frequented the village inn.

In the spring of 1837 a larger number than usual were gathered round the fireside of the Blue Dragon. A fearful storm, accompanied by violent gusts of hail, swept round the house. Suddenly the door burst open, and a young man entered, half dragging, half supporting an old man, bent and shrunk with age and infirmity. 'Here you are, sir,' he said to the old man; 'this is the Blue Dragon. You won't find a snugger berth between here and Plymouth'; so saying, he thrust the old man into a chair by the fire, and continued, half aside to the company, 'Found the old cove wandering about the cliffs, and thought he would be blown over, so offered to guide him here. I think he is a little—' and he tapped his forehead significantly. The rest of the party turned round curiously to gaze at the stranger, who, seeming to wake from some reverie, proceeded to order something hot both for himself and his self-constituted guide. The hot gin-and-water seemed further to rouse him, and he began asking a few questions concerning the country and neighbourhood; but in the very act of speaking his attention was suddenly arrested by the sight of the glass case and skeleton hand. He sprang from his chair with a savage cry of mingled terror and dismay. 'The hand,' he cried, 'the hand! why does it point at me? I never meant, O God!—' and he fell down in a fit, rolling and gasping on the floor, and shrieking wildly at intervals, 'The hand, the hand!' They raised the wretched man from the floor and laid him on a bed, whilst the doctor was hurriedly summoned. Meanwhile the sufferer continued disjointed mutterings, till, becoming exhausted, he sank into a stupor. On the doctor's arrival, however, he once more roused himself, and asked in a quieter and more composed manner whose the hand was. On being told, he trembled violently, but said: 'I am Captain Sinclair; I knew the wedding-day; I told my ship to sail without me from Plymouth, saying I would rejoin her at Falmouth. I meant to bring Anne with me; I hid in the garden, she came into it alone, I rushed forward, threw a shawl I had ready over her head, and carried her away; she resisted with all her might, but I was a strong man, and her cries were stifled by the shawl. Of course I could not get along very fast, and presently I heard voices of those in search of her. She heard them also, and made another frantic effort to free herself. My strength was nearly exhausted, but mad with rage and disappointment, I drew my knife from my belt and stabbed her to the heart, crying fiercely, "I have kept my oath, you shall never be another's." Then I hurled the body down the cliff, where I saw it catch in a crevice of the rock. O God!' he cried, shuddering and covering his face with his hands, 'I see it now – that dreadful scene, the blue waves dancing beneath the brilliant sunshine, and that white shapeless mass caught in the frowning cliff with one arm sticking stiffly upwards. I rolled down one or two stones, endeavouring to conceal it; and when I left the spot, all I could see was a hand pointing at me.' Here the miserable wretch broke off with a deep groan. In a moment more he sprang up with another wild shout of 'The hand, the bloody hand!' and so shrieking, his body fell lifeless to the ground. . . . The skeleton hand in the adjoining room was dripping blood.

THE END

ROOTS OF EVIL: BEYOND THE SECRET LIFE OF PLANTS BY CARLOS CASSABA

Long before the publication of 'The Secret Life of Plants', writers of vast imagination had seen that there was more to plant life than met the naked eye – that plants are capable of thought, of passion, of hate, of action, of striking terror in the strongest heart ... ROOTS OF EVIL is a spine-tingling collection of creepy tales by such writers, a powerfully convincing argument that plants are more alive, more aware than we think.

Read, then, the twelve stories in this book, stories that will sow the seeds of doubt in your mind ...

0 552 10072 9   50p

DRACULA UNBORN BY PETER TREMAYNE

'The man looked desperately around him, vainly seeking some escape, and then he raised his eyes to mine. No longer did his eyes burn with malevolent seductive fury; now they were glazed and despairing and filled with strange grief.

'Help me!' he sobbed. 'Help me! In the name of your great sire, in the name of the blood that flows in your veins, in the name of Dra ...'

Yet before he could finish what I did not want to hear, the burly villager had stepped forward and, with his entire weight behind him, thrust the iron spikes of the pitchfork straight through his eyes, and the man, thus impaled, fell backwards to the ground, writhing and shrieking horribly, his legs kicking as the villager leaned forward even further, pressing down on the pitchfork, finally impaling the man's head to the ground while, to my horror, the blood that spurted from the sockets shot upwards like a geyser, saturating those who stood nearby ...

0 552 10581 3   70p

REIGN OF TERROR 1 EDITED BY MICHEL PARRY

'That the sixty-four year reign of Queen Victoria generated more than its share of horrors, no one can deny. The backstreets of Victorian London, those grim, overcrowded warrens of despair, were a bustling breeding ground of horror ... If this collection helps in some way to vindicate Victorian supernatural and horror fiction and return it to its rightful position of pre-eminence, I shall be well pleased. But to be honest, my principal aim in compiling these stories is somewhat more modest. Like Dickens' Fat Boy, "I only wants to make your flesh creep..."'

From the introduction by Michel Parry in this first volume of scalp-tingling tales and macabre classics.

0 552 10335 7   65p

THE SKULL OF THE MARQUIS DE SADE
BY ROBERT BLOCH

Once it held the most evil brain on Earth ... now it was a curiosity for collectors – a sinister-looking but harmless piece of polished bone, resting on a desk ...

But somehow, something happened to whoever owned it – or bought it – or stole it ...

And each in turn discovered – in the last seconds of his life – the secret of the SKULL OF THE MARQUIS DE SADE.

0 552 10234 2   50p

A SELECTED LIST OF HORROR STORIES PUBLISHED BY CORGI BOOKS

☐ 10402 7	PSYCHO	*Robert Bloch*	60p
☐ 10486 8	ATOMS AND EVIL	*Robert Bloch*	60p
☐ 10234 2	THE SKULL OF THE MARQUIS DE SADE	*Robert Bloch*	50p
☐ 10072 2	ROOTS OF EVIL	*ed. Carlos Cassaba*	50p
☐ 09802 7	THE VAMPIRE: IN LEGEND, FACT AND ART	*Basil Copper*	50p
☐ 10335 7	REIGN OF TERROR 1	*ed. Michel Parry*	65p
☐ 10390 X	REIGN OF TERROR 2	*ed. Michel Parry*	70p
☐ 10410 8	THE RIVALS OF DRACULA	*ed. Michel Parry*	65p
☐ 10465 5	THE RIVALS OF FRANKENSTEIN	*ed. Michel Parry*	70p
☐ 10389 6	THE HAUNTING OF HILL HOUSE	*Shirley Jackson*	65p
☐ 09825 6	THE SATYR'S HEAD	*ed. David Sutton*	40p

All these books are available at your bookshop or newsagent, or can be ordered direct from the publisher. Just tick the titles you want and fill in the form below.

CORGI BOOKS, Cash Sales Department, P.O. Box 11, Falmouth, Cornwall.

Please send cheque or postal order, no currency.
U.K. send 19p for first book plus 9p per copy for each additional book ordered to a maximum charge of 73p to cover the cost of postage and packing.
B.F.P.O. and Eire allow 19p for first book plus 9p per copy for the next 6 books thereafter 3p per book.
Overseas Customers: Please allow 20p for the first book and 10p per copy for each additional book.

NAME (Block letters) ....

ADDRESS ....

(JAN '78) ....

While every effort is made to keep prices low, it is sometimes necessary to increase prices at short notice. Corgi Books reserve the right to show new retail prices on covers which may differ from those previously advertised in the text or elsewhere.